Lucky B*stard

Christian Cianci

Never Let the Bastards Win.

For everyone I love. & of course Pastor Matt.

Contents

CHAPTER 1

SHRINKS

I'm a total manic. I just want to get out of the way before we start. Technically, in my "file," I'm labeled as Conduct Disorder. That's what they call juveniles who like to do fucked-up shit. If I was ever arrested again as an adult, I'd be considered a sociopath to "the system." Whatever that is.

Have you ever been fired from your therapist? Well I got fired twice. The first guy completely flaked on me. He wouldn't return my phone calls or renew my medication. He had me on Risperdal, Vistirol, and Cymbalta. Talk about a crazy combination. He finally transmitted a message to me through his secretary. I could hear him tell her what to say in the background.

"I'm sorry Lucas, Dr. Hubshner can no longer have you as a patient."

"Why?"

I asked her with the "you've-got-to-be-shitting-me" tone in my voice.

"All I can say is he wishes to no longer have you as a client, goodbye." (Click)

I never heard from the guy ever again. Telling my parents why I needed a new doctor for the first time was an awkward conversation for them. I don't know if they knew whether to punish me or feel bad that my own therapist fired me. They opted to feel bad, although I think that's because they still had mud on their face from the first doctor they ever took me to.

I was barely a freshman in high school when I met Doctor Frank. He was an old guy with mustache, and that should have been a red flag right there. It was the very beginning of my destructive path. I had just started selling weed and getting high. My mom knew something was up right away and threw me in therapy. Through the course of talking, the doctor found out that I liked to bet on football, and had been gambling and playing poker since I was 10.

He wrote down my picks. He quickly realized I could pick winners. I found out he owned Trotter horses. Long story short, we ended up betting sports together. It went well until he told me I should hate my father. I told him he was an asshole. That night I told my parents that Doctor Frank was a degenerate gambler and that I should stop seeing him. Besides, what the fuck did I care about Trotter horses for?

That was the only time we fired one of them. When the second one let me go, everyone knew something was up. At least the second guy had the balls to tell me why I wouldn't be making my weekly drive to his cookie-cutter New Jersey suburban office anymore. Apparently, talk therapy stuff didn't really do much for me. Since he couldn't write prescriptions, he said that I wouldn't benefit from seeing him. But, he was nice about it. He referred me to my last doctor but arguably the best— Doctor Mo.

The best thing about Doctor Mo was that he taught me to not be afraid of being "different." Everyone is different, a little more, a little less, but in the end we are all ourselves and as long as you live within the lines, it'll be ok. He is the one that told me about the conduct disorder thing. He took time to educate me on what makes me, me.

I had a fucked up childhood. I can't beat around the bush on that. My mom binge-drank on the weekends and my dad was just an angry fuck. I could have sworn I had a sixth sense when I was younger because every Friday and Saturday night when my mom would drink "a little too much," I would magically wake up. As much as I wanted to stay sleeping, I was always overcome with this urge to help her. I spent many nights growing up trying to convince my mom to stop whatever she was doing and come to bed. From the start of when I would leave my room to help her to the time she would finally go to sleep, *chaos ensued in between.*

The best way to sum up my dad is with this short story.

We had only been in Jersey a week since moving from Staten Island when our neighbors finally met Dom. My hot headed, "ginzo" father. I was a mischievous little toddler and must have done something to really piss off my old man, before I knew it he was screaming. Well the neighbors were outside and apparently most people don't act like that, regardless of where you are, but in a quaint small town people take notice and take action.

Two hours later DyFus shows up knocking on my door. Talk about welcome to the neighborhood.

Depending on the audience it gets a laugh, or looks of horror. Growing up wasn't even that bad, it was just twisted. I was an only child. Not a spoiled-rotten only child, but none the less, an only child. It really is true, being the only kid kicks ass. Sharing sucks. The only downside is you only have yourself to talk to. In my opinion, siblings help shield each other from marital issues and family problems. As an only child you're always on the front lines.

I was a collared-shirt, Abercrombie ripped jean suburbanite who rocked hemp bracelets and shell necklaces. I bumped rap music out of the stereo and would get wasted drinking cheap beer, playing beer pong. I smoked a ton of pot and thought I was the man. I was a total douchebag in high school. That was me, I was that kid.

Before that, I always got into stupid trouble growing up like smashing beer bottles, breaking mailboxes and starting small fires. It seemed like every other week I was apologizing for something. I got arrested on Mischief night when I was 13 for throwing eggs at a house. I should have known then I was going to be a shitty criminal.

When I ended up on Doctor Mo's couch, I was older. He knew of all the fuck-ups I made, all the stories and friends. He was probably the first doctor I was honest with, even then I still bullshitted like 30 % of the time. He knew how to talk to me. When he told me about being pathological and what I have to look out for, in myself. He told me some of the greatest people in the world are fucked up like me. So I figured, let me just try to be more like them.

CHAPTER 2

The O'Connie Situation

The first day of any school or job is scary and nerve racking enough, but I remember the first day of my high school experience like it was yesterday, I think most people do. Even just waking up at 5:30 am, perfectly matching my clothes and making sure my hair was absolutely in place. Then walking up to the bus stop for the first time. Making sure I don't ruin my new white sneakers.

Being so anxious, I was trying to quickly pick out familiar faces and the key players that will make your day just a little bit easier. It was late summer morning where you could feel the cool autumn air settling in, letting you know school was back. I scanned the crowd at the bus stop, noticing my friend Aaron.

It's weird how friendships form. I said maybe four words to this kid the first two years in middle school. Then in eighth grade, this random kid on our bus was trying to give away these baby hamsters. He thought he bought two girl hamsters, and well 30 hairless rodent babies later left him desperately trying to pitch these fury little critters on the bus, like he was Billy Mays or something. The conniver convinced me and Aaron to take two each off his hands.

Out of that fiasco, Aaron and I became close friends, so seeing him at the bus stop helped my confidence a lot. I just remember the bus ride feeling way too short and as I saw the flagpole of the school in the distance, I knew I was only seconds away from a whole new world, a totally different experience, an experience I had been hearing about for years, and had seen depicted in movies since I was 8. I was expecting *The Breakfast Club* meets *Not Another Teen Movie*, something, you know, wild.

Walking into my new high school reminded me of walking out of the tunnel from Yankee stadium and seeing the field for the first time — it was an unforgettable experience. My school was eclectic, to say the least.

At lunch, hippies would play their acoustic guitars, skaters would hackie-sack and the delinquents could be found smoking cigarettes in the bathroom and getting high in the schoolyards beaten paths. Advanced placement kids studied on stairwells while the recluses sought asylum in the library.

Another obnoxious rant from my father comes to mind *"People around here just want to dig their heads in the sand, they don't give shit"* and the more I come to think about it, the more I think he's right. On the surface, the suburban environment is painted as this perfect picture: American flags perched proudly, complimenting their nice green lawns. Fancy-looking cars in the driveway, Parks and sidewalks. The image of success and a sense of a better life is felt instantly.

To offset property taxes they build low income housing units, some of the biggest earning gaps are in the suburbs, where you can go down any one street and see which families are better off than others, differentiating from the haves and have not's. The diversification is blatant, the haves walking side-by-side with the have not's; a girl walks by spraying her $90 perfume in her new BeBe outfit swaying her Juicy bag, while her classmate is wearing hand-me-downs and Wal-Mart specials.

I think it's there, that inquiry to the social unbalance that sparked my interest in straying from the traveled path, a personal vow to never be one of those *"people digging their heads into the sand."*

Aaron quickly became my best friend, my right hand man. Riding the bus together twice a day, and living in close proximity created a budding friendship. In all it was four of us, Mike, Kasey, Aaron and me. We had been growing up together for a while and all became close, we formed a paintball team and would sleep at Aaron's on the weekends staying up late watching his bootleg cable. They had the scrambler, it did justice. Where else can you get HBO/Cinemax for free? Plus he had constant access to a shit load of porn. It was kind of unhealthy for any family to have such an abundance of fuck flicks.

It was good times. We'd drink, get bombed, and we always knew we could sleep at Aaron's. Whenever we wanted to do some sneaky teenage bullshit. Aaron's place was our alibi.

Towards the end of freshman year, with the whole frosh stigma almost completely lifted, we all attended an end of school bang out. When you are a 15 year old boy and you hear of a party that has 2 kegs, a swimming pool, girls, and tons of hard liquor. You think you've hit the preverbal jackpot. Somewhere between standing in line to refill my red solo cup and wondering where my friends are. I realized, wow, there's drugs at this party.

I've never been to a party with drugs before.

I don't know why my mind went there but it did. When I got to the end of the keg line to refill my cup, I was told it was dry. That's when I saw Aaron, and he said *"let's get high."*

The first time I ever saw anybody roll a blunt I was in awe. I loved the smell too. As a little kid I enjoyed the smell of a skunk so this being the adult version didn't faze me. What really took me by surprise was it seemed everybody was doing it. Everybody I knew or even looked up to was smoking pot.

Immediately I started asking Aaron a ton of questions. "Where does everyone get their weed from? How much for this? What kind of bag is that?" My first time ever getting high was more of a drug dealing 101 session than a stoner circle.

I used the Aaron alibi that night with my parents. The next morning I capitalized on my new found drug dealing momentum. My ignorance had talked myself into getting a pound of midds. For all of you that don't know what that is, it's really shitty weed.

It all happened way too fast. I got high for the first time on a Friday. The following Tuesday I had pound. Was I clueless? Yes. Prisoner of the moment? Definitely. From Saturday to that

Tuesday, I must have watched Johnny Depp in *Blow* a dozen times. I thought I was the shit.

When I did finally get the weed. I was terrified of going to jail. I picked it up three blocks away from my house and ran home like Forrest Gump.

I didn't realize it would smell so much either. I stuffed three air fresheners in the bag and threw it in the back of my closet and shut the doors. I sat on my bed after that. Thinking. **Fuck, what did I just do?**

The kid I got it from, the person that basically introduced me to this new way of life, Markus. Wasn't exactly the type of person I could call up and be like.

"Uhh, I changed my mind."

That afternoon I realized I was the furthest thing from Johnny Depp in *Blow*.

Markus was my contact, my dealer, the guy and in some twisted way, a future friend. We took economics together; he was a senior when I was a freshman. The irony is ripe.

Unfortunately, as I look back, I can honestly say that meeting Markus was the beginning of the end, I pissed away my whole high school experience by getting stuck on some idea by someone I met the first month in the first year of a four year experience.

A true starting point. Being a freshman in high school who was trying to find my social niche I missed the bigger picture of how to figure out of how to climb the ladder of success and setting long term goals. I put all my focus on the wrong things.

Markus was a prime candidate for despair. A man doomed with hopelessness and too blind to see it. Being young, naïve, and just so damn ignorant I couldn't see it either. I still don't exactly know what drew me to him, maybe it was the total disregard of authority he exhibited, or it could have been the love and respect the fellow students showed him, whatever it was, I liked it, and wanted it.

What I didn't know at the time was that he spent the summer before his senior year in juvenile detention for selling drugs and aggravated assault, so the love was probably artificial, the respect was fear.

The first interaction I had with this kid was on a warm September afternoon. That day, economics was my last class. As we all waited by the door, this ogre of a kid, mammoth man child at 6 ft. 2 inches weighing a stout 270 of muscle came gorilla-strutting over to me, swaying his arms. I grew tense, a little uneasy. I was still trying to get my bearings. But before I even had time to say anything, he socked me right in the gut. Being much shorter and 140 pounds lighter, I immediately felt the blow, and pain ricocheted through me, and I dropped to the floor. The bell rang, dismissing school for the day, and the class walked out. Markus stepped over me, and that was that.

Still to this day, I can feel that punch, the force behind it, having the wind knocked out of me. It's funny to look back on it, when I asked Markus why he hit me, he simply told me,

"I saw the opportunity and capitalized on it. "

I had to stay late after school for some reason and when I went into my wallet to get a few dollars for a snack and drink, I realized all my money had been stolen from my wallet when I was at gym. My school was so grimy, when we would change for gym class, other kids would come and raid the locker room and steal your stuff. Nice right?

Anyway after realizing my predicament, I recognized Markus strutting through the hallway and took a bold chance and asked him to lend me two dollars for a bag of M&M's and a Snapple. After all, a week earlier the same kid had laid me out in the classroom with a right hook to the body that would've made Tyson proud. I felt entitled for a favor. I remember him looking at me, and without hesitation, pulling out a wad of cash that would have made Warren Buffett take notice.

"Here's 10 bucks, keep it, but if I find out you're lying to me and

actually have money in that wallet or in your pocket, I'll break your fucking jaw."

And with that, he handed me the ten dollars. Then, he reached into my pocket, took my wallet, and opened it up to make sure that I wasn't lying. So I think the instance of the money was a defining moment in forging our friendship and ultimately my plummet into a world of drugs, crime and morally fucked up situations.

My whole life I've struggled with the problem of cutting off my nose to spite my face, but no other time in my life was this more prevalent than my high school years, because back then I didn't have a clue what that cliché meant, let alone know what it meant to fail miserably hard.

It's a scientific fact that we only choose to listen and absorb 7% of all information given; the 7% I chose to soak up in high school wasn't that of teachers, scholars, or textbooks, but that of thugs, criminals, and losers, Markus being the grandmaster.

Markus and I were hanging out every day, and I not only was selling pot but also smoking a ton of it. I was a sophomore now, Markus had graduated high school, so when school would let out, he would meet me at my house and we would play PlayStation and smoke pot. A true after school special. With Markus lacking any sufficient structure, he was getting more involved, not just selling weed, but now cocaine as well, using it to support himself financially, and taking the easy way out. Instead of working for a living, he was hustling for one.

I gave the man credit, he had freedom. What I didn't see was with that so called freedom comes problems. Nothing is free in the end. His situation was sucking me in, and fast. Markus had great potential and a hard work ethic. His mind was just different though. It was almost like he was missing that one last piece of intellect or charm. He was more violent and threating than witty and charismatic.

Putting all my eggs in one basket and not diversifying my time, I was losing ground in the popularity department. I was grouped in with the trouble-makers and misfits. I welcomed the title as being cool, dark, and mysterious. In hindsight, I should've run to safer ground. **I thought I was going to have the world by its balls. Turned out it was going to be the other way around.**

Seeing an opportunity to repair my social status, about fifty of us decided to turn the newly-built park and basketball courts into a huge party. Coolers full of booze, fireworks, even an idiotic shaved headed Conan O'Brien look-alike riding a moped proclaiming the second coming of Jesus, albeit much later. This thing ended up being out of control, I watched my friend Dewey bust his tooth on a Bacardi bottle. Then proceeded to watch the tooth fall into the bottle and hear some random kid scream "THAT'S MY RAZ MAN!" Snatch the bottle out of Dewey's hand and swig the down the rest, including Dewey's tooth.

I don't remember when exactly the cops showed up, all I know is I heard someone yell

"COPS!" and I took off running. Halfway to running home, the drunken voices in my head told me "Lucas, you need to pee, and you need to pee NOW. But don't stop running." I listened and threw caution to the wind, literally. Anyway, I was supposed to have a sleepover with a few of my other friends that night: Tom, Kasey, and Dewey. Hoping that they weren't arrested, I was relieved to find them waiting on my stoop when I finally made it home. They, equally wasted as I, could see I pissed myself. Too drunk to comprehend what happened, their only words were "Dude I need to lay down."

When my mom saw all of us passed out on the couch and confronted me. I re-iterated the story I corroborated in my mind.

"We played basketball all night, I had 15 points, Tom had 23, and Kasey had 5". When asked why the whole house smelled like piss and why I'm soaking wet, obviously from urinating on myself, I

glanced back at her and simply stated, "It was an intense game Ma."

I thought I would feel guilty about getting caught. I was more embarrassed than anything. After a little heart-to- heart and stabbing her disappointment in me, my mother asked my friends to stay and she cooked us all breakfast.

One of the best lessons I ever learned from her, life's too short to be angry, live with regret, or carry on a grudge, because in the grand scheme of things, there is always something worse and more pressing to stress over, or somebody in a worse situation than you that would give their left arm to have the life and opportunities you are afforded in life.

I was taking this all very lightly, bragging and boasting of escaping the long arm of Johnny law, exaggerating stupid run-ins with the police to sound more like a hard ass. I was proud to call Markus a close friend, often enabling his criminal conduct. I was embracing the outlaw type of image.

One afternoon, we were cruising in Markus' car. We were both tired from the day, and I had accompanied him on his drug runs. Usually, we would always go back to my house, but on this specific day, my mom had taken a personal day. So we were forced to find another spot to hang at to smoke and unwind.

I remember calling up Aaron, he lived by me so it was convenient. He enjoyed smoking pot as much as anybody and his parents were very liberal, borderline hippie types who allowed him to get high in the house. Sometimes his dad even gave him weed. Markus knew him through me, so he felt pretty safe going there.

This kid O'Connie would always follow Aaron home from school and they'd chill out playing video games. Aaron usually smoked pot, while O'Connie sucked down Marlboro Reds like it was his job. Strangely, he always declined to get high. As I walked Markus in, I explained to him who the strange, nappy bearded Goth kid was that would probably be in the corner playing Grand

Theft Auto. I told him, do not fuck with this guy, just leave him alone and pay him no mind.

Walking into that house you're blasted at door with a distinct odor of old burnt marijuana mixed with the thick smoke of tar-filled cigarettes in the air. The house had a very 1970's feel to it, with the plastic on the couches in one room, the puke orange shag carpet lining the stairs and continuing throughout the second floor, the sticky linoleum kitchen floor and the stench of a wet dog overwhelmed all the five senses. Once in Aaron's room, we were exposed to the situation I had laid out to Markus just moments before. Hesitant and creeped out, Markus settled onto the bed and grabbed Aaron's bong, threw him a Dutch and a little bud and ordered him to roll it. Within minutes, we had sparked a nice sized blunt and all took a few quality bong hits.

We were feeling good. As we were all zoning out talking pot gibberish and sharing stoner theories when Markus turns to O'Connie with heavy eyes and asks

"Hit this, it's free and probably the best weed you'll ever smoke."

Always trying to hype up his product, he persuades O'Connie to take a few hits and gets the kid high. I mean, HIGHHH. Harmless we all thought.

After smoking we all lit a Newport, O'Connie his Marlboro Red. Shortly after Markus received a work call, and had to leave. Since Aaron was up the street from me, I told Markus to go ahead and that I'd walk home in a little bit. After I walked Markus out, I went back up the stairs and opened the door to Aaron's room.

The next few minutes all seemed like a blur. Within seconds of entering the room, O'Connie went to get up and use the bathroom, looking very pale and uneasy. We cracked a few jokes thinking that this kid was about to puke his brains out from getting so high. Instead as he walks into the bathroom down the hall, we hear a loud bang, like someone punched a wall. Thinking O'Connie fell, we poked our heads out to find him sprawled out on the floor. Our initial reaction was that of laughter.

We found it funny as hell that this kid got high and passed out. I threw out a

"DOWN GOES FRAZIER!"

At the top of my lungs, while standing over O'Connie, giving him the ten count.

We were laughing our asses off, then suddenly, he started to foam at the mouth. Aaron and I looked at one another. WHAT THE FUCK MAN?!

We broke out in panic. O'Connie starts shaking while spitting up foamy puke. We thought he was about to die. Then we realized Aaron's mom was going to be home in twenty minutes.

All gears shifted from O'Connie's death watch to the, "oh shit my mom's going to be home" watch. I know it sounds fucked up but Aaron didn't want his mom to find this kid jiving on the floor.

On top of everything else, O'Connie's mom kept blowing up his cellphone too! It was getting to the point where I could see Aaron toying with the idea of leaving him in the woods. I just kept thinking. *What the fuck.*

I went to get a cold compresses and when I came back in, I caught Aaron rolling O'Connie in a rug to get him out of there. I'd be lying if I said that wasn't a good idea. Just the thought of flinging this kid out of the house and carrying him into woods made me laugh insanely loud. Actually seeing Aaron try it made it even funnier. I may have been laughing hysterically in this kid's face, but I did help get some of the vomit out of his mouth while doing it.

By this time it was right around five pm, I had baseball practice, Aaron's mom was coming home any minute, and as we peered out Aaron's bedroom window we could see O'Connie's mom walking up to his house. Presumably wondering why her son wouldn't pick up her calls. If she only knew her innocent little chain-smoking, video game addicted boy was foaming at the mouth and swelled up like a gusher.

At first, I tried to figure out how to buy some time. I thought maybe we should call his mom and say her son walked to 7/11. Then I thought, maybe I should just leave. That's when I told Aaron I was getting the fuck out of there. I booked it out the back door. The whole time while I was trying to leave Aaron's house, he kept pleading with me.

"Bro you can't go, I need your help, please Luke, please, don't leave me."

His eyes filling up with tears, shaking out of fear, I simply looked at him with the same scared expression, shook my head and said "Sorry bro," and bolted out the back.

About forty five minutes later, I was fully dressed for practice, still stoned out of my mind. My dad took me to practice and drove past the house I was at an hour earlier. We saw an ambulance and about a half dozen cop cars. O'Connie was being hauled away on a stretcher.

While Aaron sat with his head against the glass in the back of a squad car. My dad slowed down to survey the scene. I kept thinking to myself. *"You're killin' me Smalls. Keep driving"*

He asked if I knew anything about this. I mean, shit, what was I supposed to say?

"Jeez Dad, I have a craziest story to tell you."

Or

"Don't tell Mom but..."

I don't know, but I opted for the **"Wow Dad that shit looks crazy,"** answer.

I didn't see Aaron until two days after that. O'Connie didn't come back to school for a few weeks. We were waiting for the bus one day after school when Aaron took me aside and told me what happened after I left. How the cops kept questioning him and what story he told, it was complete bullshit though.

He had told me O'Connie snitched out Markus. I wanted to believe him, even though my gut told me otherwise.

CHAPTER 3

High *School*

At the time of course I believed Aaron, I had no reason to second guess his story. As the bus came to pick us up, we spent the whole ride home sharing conspiracy theories and what will happen next. I must have asked Aaron a million questions on the ride home, wanting to know every aspect, to cover both myself and Markus. I was trying to get a feel if I should be expecting anything, a knock on the door.

My first moment I had alone I called Markus. I told him we had to "talk." Once in his car, I relayed the information I had gotten from Aaron. I took this all within stride. I thought this would add to my "resume." My head was completely up my ass. I felt proud I was able to escape like that, barely missing the grab from the authorities. I had a real "fuck you" attitude.

35

Markus, on the other hand, was able to see it for what it was. Maybe because he was older or had just been around the block a few too many times. He knew this was his first real major fuckup. This was only going to open the door for more scrutiny and make Markus' life harder.

Markus got pissed. He started viciously hitting the steering wheel. I was afraid he was going to set off his airbag. He just pounded the dash cursing at himself. Taken aback, and quite afraid I grew silent. That uncomfortable silence lasted until Markus turned to me and said, **"That's it, I'm done, I'm fucked, I'm going to go to jail, my life is over."**

I quickly snapped back re assuring him that wasn't true, but no matter what I said to persuade him that was not the case, he knew in his heart he was "fucked."

I stayed away from Markus for about two weeks after that. I didn't stay away from him because I saw the light at the end of the tunnel and decided to turn my life around. I wanted to protect my own ass so I didn't get arrested doing shady shit. I avoided Markus because I was trying to prolong my criminal career. I barely called him and started buying my weed somewhere else.

After a few weeks passed things started to settle down and my situation turned right back into having my daily after-school specials with Markus. I was trying to survive my sophomore year of high school.

This time it was different though, there was no more careless driving blasting the latest mix tape blowing reefer smoke. It was more sales, more movement, more awkwardness. Half the time I wouldn't even smoke with Markus. We'd drive around doing what he had to do and by the time he was done I had to go home. I ended up becoming one of his best customers, just buying twenty sacks of pot from him. That's probably how he wanted it from the start.

When I would hang with Markus every day I didn't have to sell weed because I would just get it from him, now with him frantic and always amped up on coke, his mentality changed, while mine stayed the same.

Around the same time, he started talking more about himself, and his life. This is where I heard about his mom, her re-marriage and his father's death.

Everyone has their demons, those graphic, often painful feelings and thoughts of moments in our lives that wreck us emotionally and spend the rest of our lives trying to deal with. These were Markus'. He came out of nowhere one day while we were driving on the highway,

"Right here."

I turned down the music and with a real lackadaisical response said

"Whaaaaaaaaaat?"

"My father's heart blew up in his chest, right here, past Maplewood Village Apartments. Massive fucking heart attack, I was 12 years old dude, and he drove his car into the wall. He was cheating on my mom, and was on his way home when it happened."

What do you say to someone after that? "I'm sorry?" "Dude if you need anyone to talk to?" No, you can't, the words fall on deaf ears. I've never seen a bigger, more outspoken man seem so small and humbled than when I looked back at him at that instant.

The rest of the ride was silent, with an eerie tension of vulnerability cutting through the air. Almost seeing he was embarrassed for showing weakness, I spent the rest of my time analyzing him before I got dropped off. He made a quick stop for me at 7/11, buying me a vanilla Dutch. Since I was only fifteen, I couldn't buy tobacco. He hit me off with a Newport and dub and took me home.

In the preceding weeks, things got considerably worse for Markus. He was growing increasingly paranoid and agitated. He got kicked out of his mom's house for his bad temper and the constant coming and going at weird hours due to his street life. He took refuge at a Comfort Inn off a busy Jersey highway. From there, he was doing what he wanted, without any structure or rules to follow, naturally vamping up his operation.

He concentrated fully on cocaine, flipping a few ounces a week and making daily trips to New York City. This was a recipe for disaster, if only Markus had someone older and wiser to look up to who would intervene. But he wasn't that lucky. He was a mess, no longer the friend I knew, he was a drug addict disguised as a wealthy drug dealer.

CHAPTER 4

Cops & Robbers

I stole my mom's credit

card once. Well a few times. But this one occasion was for a smoking pipe, $43 with shipping off of some stoner website. I checked the mail every day for two weeks straight hoping it would come. I hadn't been this excited for something to come in the mail since third grade when my mom ordered me a Furby.

I was so excited for this thing to come so that I could use it and show all my pot head buddies. But I was also nervous; I didn't want my parents or the cops to confiscate it, this being after 9/11 and all. Notice how I wrote parents first. Just imagine your mom's face if she walked out to the mailbox on a Saturday and stumbled across and a brown package discreetly sent from Nevada. She would think that she's the latest Uni-Bomber victim or anthrax recipient. Only to calm down and discover her fifteen year old son took her credit card and ordered a bowl off the internet and had it shipped to the house.

That was a mess I didn't want to clean up. So you can tell how relieved I was once I had this mini work of art in my hands. This thing was my baby— I took it everywhere, and its christening party must have lasted a week.

After the newness wore off, the smoking piece took its place among my possessions. Losing my fascination with it, I would let my friends borrow it. By this time, Markus was bouncing back and forth between his moms house and hotels, picking up this grandiose idea along the line of going down to South Carolina with four pounds of dirty, seedy, stemmy weed and a half kilo of cocaine and starting fresh Claiming the prices are so inflated down there, perhaps taking a cue from Biggies line *"Nicks go for 20 down south."*

He was hell bent on getting down there, planning to leave by that Presidents Day weekend. Being so caught up in his plans and seeing the potential dollar signs rolling in, he lost sight of where he was at. Whether he wasn't being aware of the consequences or felt forced into a position of immorality will always be a mystery to me. I will never understand why Markus thought that was the only way he could make "good" money.

There is a theory that states, there is no such thing as unexpected occurrences.

When something happens to you that you didn't see coming, or it feels like "it came out of nowhere," that isn't really true. We are just too distracted and forget to see the bigger picture and put the pieces together. Even though what happened seemed to come out of nowhere, it was always going to become the reality. We were just too slow to recognize it beforehand.

It was the Wednesday before Presidents' Day weekend. I got picked up from school by Markus, probably two hours before school ended. The drugs were taking its toll on him. His face looked raw.

I was in a relatively good mood because the mark of Presidents' weekend meant a long weekend away from school and a month until my birthday. The middle of February in North Jersey is one of the most depressing times of the year. It's always grey and whatever snow is left has turned into an icy black, gravel-infused mess that usually has dog piss all over it. Oh, and it gets dark at 5PM.

I only mention that because for as shitty as the landscape was, I was in an unusually happy mood. I don't know why, but turning sixteen was a big deal for me. It meant driving, not being a freshman, and it got me one step closer to becoming eighteen. All I ever wanted to do was become an adult. Being a kid to me meant having restrictions and rules. I wanted full responsibility for my decision making. *You can't limit me,* I thought.

Plus a birthday for an only child is the second greatest payday of the year, the first being Christmas. The only way it could have been better is if I was Jewish. Aaron actually, was an only child who was half Jewish and half Catholic. It's safe to say he hit the mother fucking jackpot.

Markus was always careful about not having anything "extra" on him. I had to go to a hair appointment at five with my mom and I didn't want to be stoned out of my mind around her. I was trying to get home before her so I could hide the smell of weed on me and do my usual cover up routine. Markus and I started taking rips out of my bowl speeding to my house so we didn't have to cross paths with my mom.

I'm not going to lie, I started to freak out a little. The *"whoa, I'm way too high for this situation"* kind of freak out. Markus, the persuasive super charmer he was, tried to convince me that smoking weed was something bad that should be hidden. He advocated making time for it throughout the day. It was as innocent as brushing your teeth, or taking a dump. It pops up in your day and you embrace it. He told me, don't let social taboo mind-fuck you into thinking it's wrong and that you're bad for doing it.

I was still bugging out, yet he convinced me to take one last hit before he pulled up to my house. As I am exhaling and passing Markus the bowl, my mom creeps up in her Jeep. Markus played it cool slid the bowl under his seat. I quickly popped out of his car and into my mom's. Cutting our conversation short and leaving my bowl under his seat.

On the way to my haircut, I was blazed as fuck. I lit a cigarette to hide the smell. Both my parents smoked so when they caught me for the first time it wasn't that devastating. The whole car ride was silent. My hair appointment wasn't any better. The girl who usually cut my hair wasn't there. Instead I had to sit in the barber chair of my own town's Chief Sergeant's daughter. Apparently she cut hair, who knew? I reeked of weed, and I looked like a total stoner, red eyes, droopy face, and the whole nine. I only found out she was the Sergeant's daughter because she felt compelled to tell me that piece of information. I was willing to accept half a haircut just to get the fuck out of there and away from her.

The next day, on my way home from school, I texted Markus to grab a Dutch and meet me at my house. He responded with "leaving now." As he was leaving his third floor room at the Hampton Suites, over twenty cops, detectives, and narcotics officers swarmed in on him. Catching the door before it closed, they entered his room. It took six officers to restrain and cuff Markus. They proceeded to comb the room from top to bottom, ultimately uncovering four and half ounces of cocaine, a half ounce of pot, and twenty four thousand dollars stuffed into the mattress and ceiling. They seized additional money in his bank account and confiscated his car. He was charged with Intent to Distribute; Possession of Two Controlled Dangerous Substances, a conspiracy charge and a drug paraphilia charge. My bowl was still in his car. They took him straight to jail, he couldn't make bail.

At the time no one knew what had happened, his phone was off, and people assumed he took off for South Carolina. I didn't buy it; after all, I was the one he was supposed to meet up with when he never showed.

Four months passed before I heard anything from Markus. It was a hot June day and I had the whole summer to myself. I was on AIM, bored, when all of a sudden Blazindayz420 signed on, Markus screen name.

It's been four months without any trace of Markus, and now his screen name just popped up with a message describing what had happened. He was online because he had two days at home before entering drug rehab. He was in county for the four months prior while his case was getting sorted out. If he didn't complete rehab, he had a three year sentence waiting for him on the other end. It was a very surreal conversation. In it, he outlined the nails that were driven into his coffin—the O'Connie episode.

Markus then tells me what really happened. Having seen the statements in his Discovery (evidence that is against you, that is made available to you), It turns out it wasn't O'Connie who ratted out Markus. It was Aaron. That would be our last conversation for the next two years.

CHAPTER 5

Who's Got Dubs?

In many ways, Markus sheltered me from the addicts and derelicts he would deal with. Showing me a side of life that he always portrayed as grimy, teaching me to look down on these people; they are weak and have sold their souls to get high. He was one, so he should know.

With him gone, I opened myself up to many people that had heard about me. People now wanted to get to know me. I also started selling pot again. With Markus gone, I wasn't given a steady flow of free weed and blaze outs, and buying twenty dollars' worth of pot everyday can get expensive, real quick. This also exposed me to another side of life. I was older now and I grew increasingly reckless, often making trips into the city to get enough bud to feed a steady supply back home.

This is also the time in my life where I grew up the quickest. Associating myself with older kids again earned me the nickname "the Baby." I had a bravado that I mistook for confidence. Steadily growing an inflated ego and arrogance about me, I was subconsciously grooming myself to follow in Markus' footsteps, the same steps that I criticized him for along the way.

Within my new found role in the town's underground economy, I developed relationships with a few people I had known only known previously as acquaintances. I grew up with these kids as well as playing baseball with them and attending the same school. Stan and Pita were both two years older and we had a common bond—the three of us loved smoking pot. Even though they were older, I was more advanced in the drug department, being exposed to it longer than them and carving a niche out for myself made me useful to them.

I had known Stan for a while, being on several recreational baseball teams with him, he knew my family and he was a pretty funny kid. We actually became friends because one night we were both up really late scouring the town for pot when we messaged each other asking for the same thing.

"Bro, who's got a dub?"

I'm sure that five-word phrase has sparked a lot of friendships and stories. Our story consisted of getting picked up in his 1987 eagle summit with no air conditioning at four am, sneaking out of the house leaving a makeshift dummy in my bed because my dad gets up for work around that time, we embark on a quest to find marijuana.

The journey led us outside a White Castle when the sun was about to rise. The thought process behind stalking out White Castle customers was that most people that go to White Castle are usually pretty high or intoxicated, in which case, they might be able to point us in the right direction to find the mighty green leaf. I can't say the plan worked perfectly, but we ended up getting high that night and forged a friendship.

In my mind, he was my replacement for Aaron where I would always share my weed with him and spend time with him. I began distancing myself from Aaron and a lot of other people. It was becoming more apparent to me that I was no longer looked at as just a pot-smoking jokester, but rather as a criminal that people didn't want to invite to their parties or have meet their parents out of fear that I'd bring drugs into their home or introduce them to some shady shit.

I still had a lot of friends, but my reputation was changing. It was like people could sense failure was knocking at my door. My social stock was plummeting faster than the markets during the financial crisis, I was Lehman Brothers. I kept providing fuel for the fire. Pulling bankrolls out of my pocket, bragging about dangerous situations, often exaggerating them. I loved to name drop as well, I was a total bull-shitter.

Having to surround myself with a new circle of friends wasn't difficult. Stan and I were hanging out every day. He had taken the place of Aaron nicely. Since I was losing popularity in school, I grew increasingly uncomfortable in the classroom setting. So I started skipping school more and more frequently.

Stan would always come pick me up within twenty minutes of me texting him, it was like clockwork. At first, ditching school was fun, blazing and getting Chinese food, just shooting the shit, and being able to just break free of structure was liberating.

After falling behind in my studies, I started feeling embarrassed for my choices. Skipping school wasn't just a convenient option, but more like an urgent necessity now.

I felt even more attached to Stan, especially because in my mind, I linked him to being able to leave school, like my safety net. Hanging at his house, cooped up, selling dubs, smoking pot, we found other wayward souls looking for the same thing. It's funny how misfits are always able to find each other. These were all kids who had either graduated and were lost in translation or about to graduate and had become lost in the shuffle of the world. I knew a few of them, one being a good friend of mine since middle school, Danny.

I knew Danny since I was 11, we were the same age. I knew I could trust him. He would always sleep at my house and rode the bus home with me religiously on the way home from school, having to sneak him on so he could come over, since he never had a ride down from where he lived.

All this kid wanted to be was a football player. He had great admiration for his older brother, who also played ball. Taking his number 31 jersey and reversing the numbers and rocked 13 at every game. Eventually tattooing 3113 on his back.

We all gelled as friends quickly; probably because we all loved smoking pot. I'll admit it's not the best way to base friendships on, but it worked for us. Danny, my friend from middle school, along with Stan, who became my new best friend at this point, Jason Pita who would rival Stan as my best friend, and two girls, Jessie and Jaimie.

We all became inseparable, being bound together by pot but tricking ourselves into thinking it was so much deeper than that. The girls were sexy, and everyone wanted to be the one to "hit that." Jessie always had a romantic love interest in someone outside the group, usually one of our friends.

Jaimie on the other hand was a huge flirt, very charismatic. She always knew what to say to make you feel special. She had a way with words, I swear you could never win an argument with this one, even if you were 110 percent right, she would somehow get you to admit defeat and you would apologize.

A few of us had a crush on Jaimie. They all admitted it to me, separately. Each on a different occasion, it was kind of funny actually. They all started the conversation the same way. Don't tell such and such. It always made me laugh why they trusted me with that information. I guess because they thought I was the goofiest and least likely one for Jaimie to fall for, they felt comfortable telling me. I'm not going to lie, I agreed with them, I am pretty goofy, besides at the time she was dating Pita's best friend Ryan, so I knew she was off limits.

Jason Pita. We all called him by his last name Pita. It just rolled off the tongue better, we all had nicknames. Because of Stan's big head and lack of facial expressions and features we'd rotate the names Pumpkin Head and Cool Cat to tease him. I was still the "baby."

Cool Cat and I had been buying and selling pot together for a few months already when we befriended Pita. His problem was that every time he would try and get a substantial amount of weed, he would either get robbed or beaten up badly, either way, he needed protection and a source. Stan and I saw an opportunity, just like when Markus socked me in the gut. We saw an opening and took it.

To prove his best interest was in our heart, I arranged an ambush for the kids who robbed him, getting back his lost money. I then started fronting Pita ounces on consignment, making both of us profits while cementing "trust."

I was growing more and more rogue, thinking I was James Dean or something, rather than some sixteen-year-old attending school dances and shit. I was barely enrolled in school anymore, I was now taking a full on nose dive.

At first my parents had embraced my new friends, letting me invite them over for parties and what not. As evidence of the slide began to show, the school began calling my mom about the horrible, incomplete grades, and my attitude. I became overrun with anxiety not knowing how to stop this self-destructive decision making. Every day I was digging a deeper and deeper hole that I couldn't pull myself out of.

My actions had put me in shit up to my neck. I was one string away from being completely cut off from my family, my home, my bed. It all started to unravel. It's funny that it takes a lifetime to earn someone's trust, but it only takes an instant to lose it. I was learning that lesson the hard way.

I was completely selfish. I put more stock into the relationships I forged on the street than those of the people that I had known my whole life. I was heading for the same fate as Markus. It felt like my brakes were cut and I could not stop.

Even though I started Pita off, he soon surpassed me in how much he was selling. Seeing unlimited profit, he quickly expanded by taking on new cliental and letting other kids into our group. It didn't bother me too much, I was still doing my thing, and got to party at Jessie's every weekend, which made you feel like a fucking rock star because she had a huge house. Her dad worked with NASCAR and spent the weekends traveling with the circuit, leaving her mom at the house, often giving Jessie the green light to throw parties.

The only thing that bothered me with the addition of outsiders was the persona they brought with them. They were all grimy, shyster-types, and exactly the kind of people Markus warned me about.

They always gave me a queasy feeling in my stomach. I've learned that your first instincts are usually always right on the money, and you should never doubt them. Intuition is real.

If only these kids put half the effort they did into finding drugs and getting high as they did into their education, then maybe they'd be attending Ivy League schools instead of prison.

All in all, everybody turned a blind eye to it, if the situation wasn't broken then why try to fix it? We were having fun. We thought we had this shit figured out. All appeared fine on the surface, but differences started to surface.

Stan started hanging with Pita and the outsiders all day long. Going to the liquor store and getting wasted before noon. Twisting up blunt after blunt, sucking up all the fresh air, replacing it with weed and cigarette smoke. You choked on all your senses upon entering his room, which looked more like a drug den at this point than a cool spot to sit and smoke while watching TV. Since he was enjoying getting sloshed before lunch, Stan was no longer able pick me up from school.

I had no way to escape school for the day, forcing me to look elsewhere. It wasn't too hard to find Stan's replacement, because right around this time my friendship with Jaimie started taking shape.

My whole life I've always have been able to bond with woman better than men. The three of us had known each other for a while, but I had always

59

kept my distance because all my friends were obsessed with Jaimie. With no real incentive to strike up a friendship with them, we were just casual acquaintances for a while.

One day though I saw my friend Nick in the hallway, he invited me to come along with him and said he was getting picked up by the girl from Valley High, which was in a nearby town. When I got to the green Honda Accord with an Irish shamrock bumper sticker on it, I didn't realize who was driving. I was more occupied getting caught by security. After I settled down, introducing myself as Luke, a squeaky very feminine voice answered back.

"I know silly, its Jaimie. Jessie's friend?"

Having a chance to hang out with Jaimie away from my immediate group of friends was a great relief. They would all try to jockey for her time and attention. She was the girl that you always wanted to talk to but just couldn't find the right words to say. I knew the time was right.

I embraced my time with Jaimie. Plus knowing how my friends felt about her made her that much more attractive. I knew it was wrong and would never work, but I went for it anyway. That's how I roll. *Thank you, Nick for letting me skip school with you.*

Being close with Jaimie automatically meant being close with Jessie. Besides with Stan drinking all day and hanging with Pita's friends, I needed a daily social outlet, so I welcomed this opportunity to be the third wheel.

I started to fall for Jaimie about a month before my 17th birthday. Markus had been gone a year already and it felt like life was going by so fast. As a child I could never wait to grow up, with such anticipation one would have thought I might have handled the growing pains better.

With the ripples in the pond being felt with the splash of the new blood, I kept my distance from Stan, Pita, and Dan. They were spending too much time with these kids. I was better than those kids, those drug addicts I thought. I'd labeled them as marked and left them for goners.

Suddenly nothing was as important as chasing the high.

I had slightly less fucked up daily routine. Jaimie, who was a senior and a year older than me, would pick me up from school around lunchtime and we would spend the rest of the day together, finding situations to get into and places to go. Smoking pot with Jaimie was a given, but the things we did with one another was the reason I kept coming back.

We would go hiking and explore the woods for hours. Eat junk food and drink coffee. Lots of coffee. Besides being in nature and driving around the state of New Jersey for hours. We never did anything spectacular. That was ok though, I just loved spending time with her and getting away from where I didn't want to be.

Since Jaimie and Jessie were best friends, Jaimie knew Diane, Jessie's mom, and she would let Jaimie come and go as she pleased. We'd pull up the long curvy driveway, park under the basketball hoop and walk in this magnificent doorway, adorned in mid evil architecture, gargoyles staring at you. A marvelous sight. Then, if I was lucky, Diane would be at the kitchen counter. Which was also a marvelous sight.

I had always rumors that Jessie's mom had a habit of sleeping with Jessie's guy friends. Casually picking one off here and there. A true Desperate Housewife. She has everything anyone could ever want and turns out she gets off to 18 year old fresh meat. So in my mind, I always told myself, if you ever meet this lady, make a lasting impression, because it might get you laid.

Jessie would get home and within seconds entering the house, almost on cue, she and Diane would get into screaming arguments. Quickly killing my sexual feeling for her mom, and focusing my attention back on Jaimie. Allowing Jessie to calm down for a bit and settle in from the school day, the three of us would then gather on Jessie's trampoline or in Jaimie's car, depending on the weather and spark an after school blunt.

Between the two, Jessie was the social workhorse who would provide Jaimie with all the juicy gossip, gushing out all the details of some scandalous affair and highlighting the weekend's events, which "everyone" was going to. Jaimie then would relay the information to me, so when we'd all sit around getting high, talking, I would know what the hell is going on.

It felt good hearing other people's dilemmas and mindless bullshit. With all the problems, I was creating for myself, I welcomed anything to take my thoughts off it and help me bury those god awful feelings.

What made me start falling in love with Jaimie was the innocence we were both trying so desperately to hold onto. Stan boozing his life away, Pita and Danny getting hooked on freebase and heroin. We found the laughter and kindness lacking in our lives in each other. We kept our dealings as confidential as possible. Only including Jessie in our relationship status, we had to. After all Pita and Danny were head over heels for this girl and my best friends, regardless of their current situations.

No one would have understood, and since our relationship started around the time of my unraveling, my mother largely blamed Jaimie as a main influence. Knowing she could never come over for a Sunday dinner, and at the cost of igniting backlash from Danny and them it was just easier to keep our relationship in house. It added a sexual dirty little secret vibe when we saw one another. Which made it that much more intense. I was leaning on Jaimie more and more, using her as my crutch.

I remember one day I was called into the principal's office. Thinking it was for my spotty attendance record or poor grades. I wasn't sweating it, I figured I'd feed them some bull, take my lumps and return back to class, leaving school shortly after that. I opened the door to Mr. Strawberry's office, our block-headed principal who got his rocks off being an authority figure to minors. To my dismay, I was greeted by Detective Sanchez and Detective PaChunka, the towns leading narcotic officers.

"Hello Luke, I'm sure you know we are. It was only a matter of time before we met buddy. Mr. Strawberry was surprised you showed up today, we were starting to think you were too cool for school."

Taking a seat on the closest piece of furniture, my calm persona was now doused with a cold bucket of reality. A look of emptiness jumped on my face, Sanchez looks down at me and said...

"We would like it if you came with us, I have a few questions I'd like answered, and this isn't an invitation to talk, it's an obligation."

Just like that, I was handcuffed and led out of school. Placed in the back of an unmarked squad car and hauled away to the station to face a blast of questions and accusations. Left alone in the backseat of that car with only the smell of cheap leather and stale throw-up, I was flooded with emotions. The obvious feelings of fear and anxiety, accompanied by the sweaty palms, the rush of adrenaline, and dry mouth all occurring simultaneously.

I couldn't escape the feeling of pride I felt though. Focusing on the notion of look what I did, all this fuss and commotion over me. I was deemed important enough to not be taken lightly or over looked. I was delusional. I saw this as another story to tell. Adding another notch to my resume of mayhem. It felt like I had just been recruited by a top advisor from Princeton or something, having someone take notice of my work, but this wasn't a professor, but two drug cops that don't have patience for bullshit.

For the latter part of two hours I was handcuffed and placed in their integration room. I looked at this as more of a game or challenge than a chance at help. Constantly blowing off their inquiries and skirting any question I felt threatened my freedom. I was protecting low-life scumbags, gambling with my future so I could preserve theirs. Such a twisted outlook. Having made such poor choices and decisions leading up to all this, it felt like the norm to just keep making them. After every dead end answer I gave, they would just stare at me in disgust and frustration. I thought it was the frustration of not getting the answers they were looking for but it was aimed more at me. They were disgusted that a talented young man like me would choose such a seedy, unbecoming path.

I emerged from the cold integration room a free man, not charged with anything. I walked down the hallway and standing in the entrance way of the police station was my parents, a look of disbelief and disappointment plastered on their faces. I winced in the agony of knowing that I had to explain all this. Anyone with parents knows whenever their "disappointed" it's worse than the wrath of their anger. I must have heard the word disappointed at least a hundred times during that ten minute car ride back to the house.

My father was always the yelling dictator within our family nucleus, my mom being the calm level headed one. His temper and erratic driving always scared the shit out of me, but there was nothing I feared more than the evangelical voice of my mother because her words were always real, and knew how to strike a chord within my heart. I also knew if my mom ever raised her voice and screamed, I had really fucked up. This woman makes it her business to always welcome rational calm conversation. So when she resorts to raising her voice, it's because you've left her no other option.

That night I curled up into a ball in my bed, I tried to make sense of it all. Why the cops chose to target me, what the impact of all this will have on my family, should I walk away? **That night, I went to bed making up my mind, today was the last time I would ever step foot into my high school.**

Even with the decision to abandon school and the situation with my parents and the law worsening. I was pumped for my seventeenth birthday, spending it with Jaimie, and finally getting my license, those car keys and picture ID represented freedom in my eyes.

At this point, Jaimie wasn't just my lover, but also my best friend. Continually relying on her as my outside friendships with good people soured due to my vigilante attitude, Jaimie kept sticking by my side as my predicament grew increasingly worse. I had already pissed away my education and was on the verge of alienating my family, but now the people I had conducting business with were about to make a move against me.

Seeing me as weak and doubting my street integrity due to my run-in with the police, a real shady character by the name of "Ty Money" tried to get me.

Henry Hill in Goodfellas said it best. *"Your enemies come with smiles, they're usually your best friends that do it to you."*

The quote rings true to me on several different levels, this time pertaining to Ty Money and his plot to rob me for more than two thousand dollars' worth of pot. At seventeen, that was basically my life savings.

This was Markus' best friend, someone Markus told me I could trust and utilize. Now this kid tried to fuck me in the ass in the most inappropriate way. He successfully conned me into trusting him with my money. By the time I saw the writing on the wall, my money long gone and the hope of scoring a large quantity of pot and an even larger pay day stolen.

That night I got in touch with a few of my people who I had promised pot to and explained the situation. In all walks of life, people will always shoot the messenger and not the message. Taking heat from my friends to take swift action, I hatched a plan of retaliation. I snapped that night and went to his house. He and his parents were inside sleeping. I walked up to his driveway with an aluminum Redline baseball bat in one hand and a seven inch Butterfly Knife in the other.

I approached Ty Money's car and proceeded to stick my knife in his two tires on the passenger side, bending his axel. Not feeling satisfied with that, I then clenched the bat with both hands tightly, my knuckles turning blue from squeezing so hard. I unleashed all my pent up rage and self-disappointment onto Ty Money's Acura. I fucked that shit up.

It must have been one AM but I didn't care. The damage I did to that car was a reflection of what I was doing to myself. Beating myself into the ground until there was nothing left except for me to gather all the little pieces.

Doing that served no good purpose, not even for the purpose of revenge. I started a grease fire and only had water to try and put it out. I was still without my money, I had no pot and now I was even deeper in over my head than if I just let it go and swallowed my pride and took a shot of humility. I treated two grand like two million. My foolish vigor got the best of me. There was a big gap in who I thought I was, and who I had become. That night epitomized it. With my birthday coming up, things were only about to get worse.

CHAPTER 6

No Brakes

You can't shit on people all year round then expect them to warm up to you on the days you want something from them. For my seventeenth birthday, I didn't even get a card. Instead I got a yellow piece of note paper. On it, scribbled. *Happy Birthday Lucas! Good luck to you as you navigate your way through life, Love Mom and Dad.*

I don't blame them one bit, I would have done the same thing to my kid if he was out of hand the way I was. I was a fucking asshole to everybody. A real cocky son of a bitch. I swear my mom has the power to pull cosmic forces in her favor because later that day I miserably failed my driver's test, only further dampening my birthday fun.

I could always count on Jaimie though to bring a little sunshine into my life. On the way home from my test, I convinced my dad to let me take out my new car that I had waiting for me in the garage. He agreed to let Jaimie drive me around. She met me at my house and before I knew it we hit the open road. I waited sixteen years and 364 days for this moment. I guess another two weeks wouldn't kill me.

We found ourselves lodged in the same circumstances were usually in, waiting for Jessie to get home from school so we could all smoke and get high. Normally, I would have celebrated with Stan, Dan and them, but I figured I'd have more fun with the girls that day. Nice car, sexy chicks, sign me up.

I was born on the first day of spring so whenever my birthday rolls around the weather is changing, some days it can be seventy and breezy, other days it's downright cold and rainy. It starts to get lighter out but is still dark by six PM. On this particular day, there was a slight chill in the air so Jaimie, Jessie, and I decided we would christen my new car in Jessie's driveway. We rolled up and sparked my birthday blunt.

After about five minutes, my car was filled with smoke, choking on the lack of fresh air, we cracked a window. Breathing in something other than weed and cigarette smoke was a good change of pace.

Turning on the dashboard lights in my Mitsubishi Coupe, the blue interior lights made us feel like we were astronauts on a space ship. It led us to phrase *"Blasting off on Apollo 420, next stop, getting as high as the moon."*

Corny I know, we were total stoners. Among three friends, we found it pretty amusing and used it as more of code talk or an inside joke. It felt like the weed we were smoking was burning forever. We found anything and everything overly funny that day. It must have been the type of pot because usually we were just mellow and relaxed, that day though if we saw a chipmunk scurry out from under a bush, we all died laughing. Whether it's because there's actually an animal called a chipmunk, it's kind of an awkward name if you really think about it. Or because I've always resembled one of those furry little creatures, they are just funny. This little guy and I definitely could have passed as cousins or something. I know the immature humor comes from getting too stoned, but what I did next was just sheer stupidity.

What seemed to be the blunt that never ended, finally gave out its last hit. We all immediately lit up a cigarette like clockwork right. Our eyes bloodshot and our motor skills greatly diminished. We decided to pull the car back up the driveway and watch TV at Jessie's for a little bit. Even though I tanked my driver's test, I was behind the wheel and bestowed upon myself to move my car from the uphill incline back up to the top of the driveway.

Somewhere between point A and B, I thought I had turned my car on. When I put the shifter in drive, instead of powering forward, I started drifting backwards! I immediately slammed on my brakes like I was avoiding a rear end collision. We were so high that we forgot we hadn't fully started the car. We convinced one another someone must have cut my brakes while we were getting high.

We were rolling back slowly. My brakes not responding, Jessie called her dad for advice, and since he worked with NASCAR, we thought it was a good idea. He finally picked up, but not before my car came to an abrupt stop by rolling and backing up into a forty year old Birchwood tree. Half my car was in a ditch, the other half backed into a tree. My first thought was, *no wonder why I failed my driving test.* Jaimie screamed her head off while Jessie's dad was on the speaker phone. The first words out of his mouth were,

"Heyyyyy Jessie? The car's definitely on right?"

Erupting in laughter out of our own stupidity, Jessie hung up the phone. Feeling like complete idiots, we pushed my car out of the ditch. I was lucky, the car only had minor scratches. We then figured we'd just drop Jessie off, sparing us the embarrassment of seeing her father who we sent out an S.O.S to only minutes earlier. Jaimie and I just headed home. If I knew this was going to be the last time I was going to see Jaimie. I probably would have done things a little differently. But since I lacked any foresight abilities. I simply waived goodbye to her, foolishly taking for granted I would see her tomorrow.

CHAPTER 7

Cool Cats

Hanging out with Jaimie and Jessie was great. But I needed some time with the boys. So I called Stan.

Stan wasn't on his A game anymore, but I still associated with him. That first time trying to find marijuana in the middle of the night had evolved over time to where he was always my go to guy. I felt that I could trust him. Sometimes while getting high in his beat-up Eagle Summit, we would have the music pounding out of the speakers too loud. Occasionally, we drew the attention of cops.

Every sticky situation I got in with him, we always somehow made it out alive. That's what further enhanced our bond. The only thing better than getting into trouble with someone, is getting out of trouble with them; you share a *moment* with that person when that happens. That's what we did

79

the best, shared moments where we knew we had each other's back.

One night we were going 60 mph in a 25 mph school zone. The town's Chief of Police was directing traffic. They occasionally do that in small suburban towns to drum up support for the force. Otherwise he would never be getting his hands dirty. Apparently he couldn't fit the bright colored safety vest mandated to wear. So he opted to conduct traffic in his navy blue issued trench coat. Smart.

Stan and I, freshly baked off our L cruise, headed toward home. We each had a Newport in our hands. Reduced to a stoner-like trance, the base from the music rang in our heads. We shoot past the Chief of Police. Not seeing him in the dense night air parlayed with the music drowning out his whistle made him invisible to us. Narrowly missing the Chief, **Stan and I continued on our way home with our heads in the clouds and buds in our pockets.**

He dropped me off. I went upstairs and stashed my weed. Still pretty high, I looked down and notice two missed calls from Stan on my cell. Before I could even call him back he shot through with another ring.

" *Dude, listen,* **don't freak out** *but I'm on my way back to your house to pick you up, I got a* **cop** *with me saying my license plate was called in by someone and needs all the occupants of the car for questioning,* **come outside**...."

Most people would be shitting themselves if they heard that. But Stan always loved to fuck with me, playing jokes telling me

"I'm outside but hurry up 'cuz there's a cop car sitting out here," or

"The cops followed me and want to talk to us about that thing you did, quick dude hurry up!"

He liked to do this because I usually kept him waiting outside for an hour or so while I got ready to go out. So this was his way of rushing me out. I didn't believe him anymore so when he said that I told him **"fuck you dick,"** and hung up the phone and turned my attention to passing the Wendy's I ate two hours earlier. I'm in the process of reliving my large combo number 4, when I hear a knock on the door.

"Hi Mam, Officer DeBlaski of the Watsessing Police Department, I need to speak to your son regarding a personal matter."

"LUCASSSSSSSSSS!!!! GET DOWN HERE!"

My mom doesn't like surprises. Hearing her anger echo through every letter of my name scared the shit out of me, literally. I rushed down stairs and out the front door.

The cop tells us we almost mowed down the Chief of Police at the football game. The police thought it was intentional. Since it was in a different town, the cop told us we had to follow him. There was a squad car trailing us and one leading in front. We couldn't move. They led us to an abandoned parking lot close to the high school. Waiting for us was about nine cop cars, fifteen officers, two dogs and one guy with his gun drawn.

I remember looking at Stan and thinking, **"Oh, fuck**, *they're going to go* **Rodney King** *on us."* I saw worry on the kid's face. First time I ever saw any other expression other than laughter on the kid who lacked facial detail. Cool Cat was shaken.

The officers surrounded the car, each looking more pissed off than the guy next to him. The situation grew tenser as there was still an unknown circling. Their formation opened up to let in the Chief. The guy we almost hit, but didn't know it. He approached the car, taking short precise steps, making his presence and power known. He towered over the car window, his flashlight peering in and shining in our eyes, he ordered us out of the vehicle.

"You didn't see me? What the hell is wrong with you? You could have killed me."

We started kissing this guy's ass. Stan and I were stepping over each other with apologies to this guy. We finally got across the message that we didn't see to him or hear his whistle. We blamed the speeding on having to get home for dinner. I tried to pitch it as a huge misunderstanding and a valuable lesson learned on our part.

It was dead silent for a good minute. Sixty seconds is a long time to wait when it has to be. Staring at the Chief, I didn't want to break eye contact. He looked around to his men, some with their guns drawn, then back at us, then them again, throwing his hands up shouting.

"God Dammit Hurwitz! I told you it was unsafe for me to direct traffic with no safety vest on! Next time order me one that fits! You gentlemen, slow down and pay attention next time, ok? My guy's going to write you a warning, be safe have a good evening."

That was the luck we had. Each time an instance like that would take place we would feed off one another. Bull shitting really is an art. I mean, we would come up with some crazy shit. I wish I could reference a situation but then I would be bull shitting about my bull shit. And that ain't right. Stan and I would probably be college graduates if it was offered as a major.

The last close call I had with Stan, we had gotten pulled over for broken tail light after just finishing a joint, and I had about four grams of pot on me. It was on December 23rd at 11:47 pm. I remember the time because once the rush of adrenaline hit me after realizing we had gotten stopped. I was immediately met with the thought.

"Oh My God, don't get arrested on Christmas Eve Mancini. "

It was a different song but same dance with us, only this time I had the feeling the cop knew. He only pulled Stan out of the car, searching only him. The cop gave me a hard time and asked tough nose questions but never once made a move over to my side, or asking me to step out of the car.

I had the four grams of pot in my right pants pocket, with the outline of the bag being visible through my jeans. I swallowed my spit hard, clenched my knees with my sweating palms, and was shaking my leg worse than a six-year-old having to pee.

I screamed guilty, but he never paid me enough attention. He let us drive off that night with giving Stan two tickets. I went back to Stan's, got high, and then we parted ways. That night I promised God, I'd never do that shit again. I realized I'm a lucky bastard.

I had known this guy by the name of Chavez for a few years. Originally, I met him through Markus. I hung out with Chavez a few times for the weed, but I quickly stopped once I saw what an out-of-control, animalistic hot head he was. This guy was fuckin' nuts. I got high with this kid one time on Halloween and in the middle of driving he slammed on the brakes. The bud went flying.

He pulled into this gas station, idled his car in a dark spot and hopped into the back of another car left idling while the guy was inside buying cigarettes. The guy came out, got in his car, and put his car in reverse when suddenly Chavez popped out from the backseat. Scaring the hell out of the guy, Chavez shoved his head against the window three times, yelling wildly as he took money out of the guy's wallet. He ran to his car and took off.

The whole time this is going on, I'm just sitting there thinking "what the fuck", what a crazy asshole. Chavez was happy like a pig in shit. He finally got the money that guy owed him. That was all I had to see to know Chavez didn't fuck around.

Desperate times breeds desperate acts and after spending the day with Stan burning L after L in his room, we decided we would ask Chavez for a spot, requesting him to front us some weed so we could sell and make money. Since I knew Chavez, it would be an easy request. The hard part was going to be selling the weed before we smoked it all.

I hated the idea of this favor because I knew how unstable Chavez was. I wanted so badly to back out. I didn't though, and Stan and I went ahead with the deal to get fronted four ounces of bud, a quarter pound for around $1,000, a decent profit potential.

Right away, we got off on the wrong foot. The first night was spent smoking, twisting up handfuls, and one cannon after the other until we nearly passed out from the billowing smoke. Putting ourselves in an early hole meant having to skimp the bags and rip some people off, which in return pissed off our client base.

Unable to sell the weed in a timely manner meant keeping Chavez waiting on his money and us with a shit load of weed that we just kept smoking since none of us had the self-control to just let it sit there.

We went to the well one too many times and it had run dry. Stan and I only had half of the $1,000 we promised Chavez. With no bud left to sell, we needed to buy time, so I met with Chavez and paid him the $500, swearing to him by next week he'd have the rest. It was a blatant lie. I knew I wouldn't have it, I figured if I was the one to bring him the first half of payment he would relax a little. I also knew he was over eighteen, which meant since I was a minor he wouldn't touch me in public.

Everything I touched was turning to shit, I couldn't catch a break. What made me think my next scheme would work out any better still puzzles me to this day. I was stressing this Chavez thing hard. I was at my breaking point, but I was too stubborn to give up. I pressed further.

This was affecting me a lot worse than it was Stan. He took this with a grain of salt, not paying Chavez's threats any mind and never entertaining the idea of getting hurt. It seemed as if Stan dug his head in the sand, he was really just in a drugged-out daze most of the time.

I didn't want to screw over Aaron. We were still friends, even after the Markus thing. I just needed money, and knew I could rob his house. As fucked up as that sounds, it's true. If he never found out about it, I was planning on still hanging out with him.

I finally got my license two weeks after my birthday. I was finally able to drive my car without hassle and obtained the freedom I'd coveted so much. Somewhere between staying out till the wee hours of the morning and sleeping to four PM, I devised the plan to enter Aaron's house.

Stan and I were to stalk out the home, watching to make sure everyone had left and no one was inside. Once everyone left by 8:30 AM, I was to climb the fence to their dog run by hopping over and crawling through the doggy door.

89

I walked up to the fence that spring morning with a knot in my stomach that felt like a forty pound stone. Breathing heavily, I jumped over the fence, landing in a pile of dog shit. As soon as I got inside the familiar smells of Aaron's house smacked me in the face. His dog Sammy greeted me as if I was a welcome visitor. *Not this time though buddy.*

Even though I knew no one was in the house, I spazzed every time I heard a creak in the floor boards or thud from the wall. Stan was at the back door waiting for me to let him in. I opened the door and reiterated to him to be quick. From there the hunt was on, ransacking their DVD collection, raiding their jewelry box, pocketing an IPod, a Mont Blanc pen, and emptying their trays of change. If we saw it, we grabbed it.

We were only in there for maybe twenty minutes tops, but it felt like an eternity. We gathered our spoils and left out the back door, locking it behind us. Breaking into a house and burglarizing it is just as scary for the thief as it is for the victim. **I've been on both ends, and can say there is fear on each side.**

After we made our getaway, we started moving the goods. The change was cashed, and DVDs traded in. We then made our way down to Newark to pawn the gold jewelry.

On the way down to Newark, I rolled up some weed in a cigar I had taken from Aaron's house. We smoked and talked about going back and breaking in around Christmas time to steal all his presents.

We were two pasty white kids roaming around the slums of Newark trying to pass off stolen jewelry. Needless to say, we stuck out like sore thumbs and resembled crack heads more than high school students.

Right away, our hopes were dashed. The first gold-buying shop took one look at all this chintzy, shiny, yellowish metal in this crinkled zip lock bag and told us flat out, this isn't real. It was fake, fugazee, costume jewelry.

Not only did we manage to steal fake jewelry, but I had robbed my old best friend to do it. Embarrassed by what the owner said, Stan and I

91

walked out. We settled for nothing, jetted back to my car, and hopped onto 280.

On the way back, I instructed Stan to toss the fake jewelry out the window. I did not want to bring that stuff back into town. Making one more stop before I dropped Stan off, I decided to check the value of a ring I took from Aaron's mom's jewelry box. We walked into a local silver and gold pawn shop and asked to check the ring's worth.

I should have known right then that something wasn't right, but I was too high to realize. As soon as we walked in, I could feel the attention in the room shift to us, the owner's eye-balling us. I approached the counter with my inquiry.

The gentlemen took one look at the ring and asked for my ID, saying it was store policy. After jotting down a few notes, he handed me back my ID and ring. He said I had to be 21 to sell something in this store and that he couldn't make me an offer. Before I left, he asked where I had gotten the ring.

Not thinking too deep into it, I rolled some story off my tongue and walked out.

That afternoon, Stan, Pita, Danny and the crew met up at Dunkin Donuts. We picked up right where we left off. I completely blocked out the crazy shit Stan and I did only hours earlier. We acted as if nothing was wrong, easily going about our day.

Two days had passed since the Aaron robbery and I was getting Chavez's money in order to repay my debt. It was around lunchtime when I woke up. I jumped right out of bed and into the shower, eager to meet up with my friends. I was just about to lather up when I heard a loud bang at my front door and the sound of heavy boots walking up my stairs. Stopping at the bathroom. At first I thought I was getting robbed or beat up. My second thought was. *Oh, shit, the cops.*

"Mr. Mancini, this is Detective Sanchez, you have ten seconds to come out, or were coming in."

Before I could shut off the water to the shower, the bathroom door flew open and Sanchez ripped me out of the shower butt-ass naked. I honestly had no idea why this was happening. I was so fucking delusional. I couldn't put two and two together.

I was able to grab a towel before I was escorted down stairs. I was seated in my dining room next to two detectives and a patrolman. Not to mention my mother. Sanchez and his partner searched my room while the regular cop stood watch over me. I took this very lightly. I joked with the cop saying, *"Where am I going to go? Bolt out the front door in nothing but a towel? "*

The whole time I was way too calm. I thought I got one over on them and was planning on suing the shit out of them for something. I had no weed in the house and I didn't have any bowls or bongs. I kept thinking, ***"Mancini you're goooood."***

I thought they were looking for drugs. I'd completely forgot about the robbery. They were up there for a good thirty minutes until the noise from my room suddenly stopped.

Sanchez walks down the stairs with my cellphone in one hand, and an empty pot baggie with the ring I stole in the other. I still didn't think I was fucked at this point. Who gives a shit about a cellphone? They weren't going to charge me with an empty bag of pot after this fiasco. And the ring? I had a solid story. I found that shit. ·

Sanchez then threw me a curveball. He asked whose IPod this was on my phone. I told him it was mine. Truth being I stole it from Aaron's house and took pictures of it to sell it on eBay.

The next question they asked really caught me with my pants down. They wanted to search my car. I didn't even think twice when I said.

"Yeah. Of course, Officers!"

I don't know if anyone has ever consented to a search as enthusiastically as I did that day. I could have sworn the car was clean. I knew if they didn't find anything, this whole charade would've come to a close and they would've left.

It took the detectives all of two minutes to find the bag of fake costume jewelry. They came inside and dropped it on the table. Fucking Stan man. He never threw out the jewelry and my lazy ass didn't double check. I was now staring at a Burglary and Theft charge, along with Grand Larceny.

They started reading me my Miranda rights. I cut them off and asked how the hell can you get arrested for stealing fake jewelry? I meant it to be a rhetorical question, but it drew a sharp response from Sanchez.

"You would have been really fucked if this shit was real. I got news for you kid. That ring, it's a wedding band. You don't just find those lying around."

The look on my mother's face was a, I-have-no-son, I-hate-you type of look. In fact, she even said it, a few times. I was totally up shit's creek. Sanchez, who I feel like I've known half my life at this point because of all our raw conversations gave me two choices.

Choice A: Go straight to Juvenile Detention and await my court date.

Choice B: Check into a patient rehab immediately.

Granted, I didn't want to go to jail. But I also didn't want to go to rehab. I had heard horror stories about both places. All I knew was I didn't want to go to jail. So I chose B. Rehab.

After making my decision, the cops asked me if I was with anybody. I knew they knew it wasn't just me. I just couldn't bring myself around to name names. It was a pride thing. After two minutes of silence, they told me to put on clothes. I was going to rehab. That's when I knew this shit was real.

They allowed my mom to take me. She followed the squad car there. I stared at the back of it the entire time while I listened to my mom cry about my disappointment. I kind of wished the cops let me go with them. When we finally got there I broke out in a full on panic. I had already chain- smoked the whole way, but now my mind was finally adjusting to what was happening. We waited for about an hour inside. Sanchez and his partner had left, only the patrolman stood behind. The three of us were called into an empty medical room where the nurse proceeded to shut the door. After a long pause she said.

"I'm sorry but this is an adult-only center, we don't accept minors. You can go home now."

Sanchez fucked with me. He knew that place only accepted adults. Since I was only seventeen, he knew I wouldn't be admitted. His goal was to scare the shit out of me. It worked. April Fools on Mancini. He also cut me a huge break. I didn't go to jail that day and he gave me a week of freedom before my first court date.

CHAPTER 8

Good Luck Boys

I'm not going to lie to you. I thought this was all going to go away. I actually told myself "maybe they decided to not move forward with this." Can you say delusional?

About a week after the rehab scare, I got my first letter in the mail from the court. I was to appear that Friday in front of the judge. I had heard so many stories of juveniles doing fucked-up shit and getting away with little to no punishment that I didn't think twice about what could happen to me.

My parents got me a lawyer. I was personally broke so my only option was a public defender. I should have opted for the public defender because my mom's idea of getting me a lawyer was more about teaching me a lesson than making sure I got off scot-free.

The first time I met this woman, she interrogated me for a half hour accusing me of being more than just a pot head.

Her exact words were.

"People don't break into homes because they just smoke pot. "

Like what the fuck lady?

I understand that she wants to know who she is working with, but I had never done any other drug in my life besides smoke weed. I kept telling the lawyer lady I had been in outpatient rehab for six months and if she didn't believe me call the drug testing place. Heading into my first court appearance I felt like the whole world was against me. Even I was against me.

Friday's first court date ended with me being reprimanded to house arrest until my trial/plea deal. Before the judge smacked down his gavel he looked at me and said,

"Son, I don't know how you aren't in jail right now. You should be locked away, but since you aren't, I'm deeming you a flight risk and putting you under house arrest. See you in two weeks."

Ouch.

In elementary school, my dad would pick me up and we would get lunch and a pack of baseball cards from 7/11. I'd go home and he would help me with my homework. I'd be itching to get into my pajamas by five PM to watch the Simpsons and Home Improvement.

Those days were long gone though. Somewhere over the years, I lost the ability to just be. I'd grown to always needing to be doing *something*. As I got older that *something* needed to be some kind of excitement. High school was my first real taste of excitement. I just didn't know how to handle it.

It used to be so simple. Growing pains are hard, but I was making them way harder than they needed to be. I had some great memories with my family, even if some were formed from twisted circumstances. Now the only time I spoke with my parents was during the car rides to the lawyer's office. **I swear, I'm the grand master of wasted moments.**

I bring that up because one would think with being confined to my house. I'd be able to make up for lost time. Yeah, no. I fucked that up too. I couldn't stand being home. I tried to violate house arrest every chance I could.

Look, I felt like a total loser. I hadn't finished the tenth grade, I had a nasty pot habit, and my parents and friends hated me. I was empty inside, but I was too scared to admit it and created a false bravado to help me deal. I would sneak out of my house at night to smoke pot with Stan and Pita. *That's* what I risked going to jail for.

During the day, my grandmother would "watch" me, until my parents came home. Being under house arrest, you aren't allowed to be left alone. Both my parents worked so we had my mom's mom, who my dad hated, stay with us. She was known as Brooklyn Nanny.

Here's the deal with Brooklyn Nanny. She was an old Irish/German woman who didn't take shit and hated Italians, my father most of all. I touched earlier on my dad Dom. Brooklyn Nanny thought he was a lying, cheating, two-bit scumbag with a drug problem. One Thanksgiving, she got so mad at Dom, she threw gravy on him and said

"Fuck you! You, Guinea Bastard."

There is a City Nanny too, but she just sat there.

Brooklyn Nanny brought an additional layer of tension in the house besides me being an arrested criminal. One day, I was going in the front yard to play one-on-one stick ball with Stan when before I walked out she told me,

All my other grandchildren are doctors, lawyers or aspiring ballerinas. You're just a criminal.

I thought to myself. *Thanks Nan.*

After setting up a beach chair as our strike zone and packing a lip of Mint Skoal to get me in the baseball mood, it was on! Stan ended up whooping my ass, but I didn't care because I was pouring sweat. I knew I'd be able to get right to sleep that night due to the workout. I slept like a ton of bricks that night.

Around eight AM the following morning, my mother barged into my room. She abruptly shook my body.

"Get up, Get up NOW!"

She yelled at me.

I responded with,

"Shouldn't you be at work? Its 8:30 in the fuckin' morning. "

She snaps back with,

"The court called me on my way to work. You have to be there by **9:30 AM***. Your father will meet us there."*

My court date wasn't supposed to be until Friday, and now all of sudden, they couldn't wait to see me? I immediately knew this wasn't good. My mind was racing. I pounded a pack of Newport's on the way there.

I knew I had violated house arrest, but did they? And if so how? The phone didn't ring yesterday, and whenever I went out, it was late at night.

We pulled up to the courthouse, the area under my arm pits drenched in stress sweat, leaving my white shirt in a pool of yellow perspiration. My dad was out front chain-smoking like I was. As I walked up to him he greeted me with the phrase,

"You're fucked you know that? They called yesterday around 1 o clock, and no one answered the phone or called them back, that's **violating** your house arrest Lucas."

Whether my grandma didn't answer the phone, or I was caught unknowingly one night outside will always be a mystery to me. In the end, it didn't matter though. This was on me. My dad was right. I was fucked.

My lawyer, quick to spare no sympathy shared the state's view of breaking into someone else's home with me. Basically it goes like this. If you break into someone's house, we are going to throw you in our house, which is Jail.

She went on to tell me that if I chose to go to trial, I would be tried as an adult, if I was found guilty, I would probably end up in prison. Whether or not this is true, this is what my lawyer told me. It scared the shit out of me.

When I say scared. I'm talking about true fear. People talk about epiphanies and the moment it all started to make sense. Well I was having the opposite of that. I'd just kamikazed my life.

As I was walking into the courtroom, I already knew I'd self-sabotaged myself all the way to juvenile detention.

"ALL RISE FOR THE HONORABLE JUDGE SHATNER"

His deep, tenor-like voice made the hair on the back of my neck stand up and my heart palpitate. I was intimidated. I also wasn't dressed for the occasion. I wore beat-up white Jordans, corduroys, and an Abercrombie & Fitch shirt with a fugazy cross/hemp necklace. I should have worn a suit.

"Due to the nature of your crime, and the violent acts it entails, I have no

mercy in the fact that this is your first offense and sentence you to Juvenile Detention immediately for the maximum ninety day term for a juvenile. You are to be transferred to Merseyside Village Treatment Center once they have space to accept you, whether that is before or after your ninety days end."

His gavel pounded the podium. It acted as the period to the end of his sentence. I was ordered to take off all my jewelry. I was property of the state now.

I was then escorted down to get my finger prints taken and start the intake process. The first thought I had when I started walking was,

"Wow, shackles are painful."

Joking aside, I was a total zero at this point. As I'm getting my finger prints taken, I glanced over my shoulder and caught a glimpse of my family being ushered away, devastated and in tears. I died a little bit on the inside when I saw that.

Honestly, in the moment I compartmentalized everything. I've blocked 95% of it out. Not by choice, I think my survival instincts had begun to kick in. I was about to enter a completely different world.

That world started in the basement of the court house in the holding cells where they keep you before your transfer to jail. The guard opened up this big blue steel door and nudged me into the cell. I had two other flunkies there waiting for me.

On the walls were names and initials etched into it, two big initials stood out and over powered the rest, A.S. in big, gaudy child-like writing covered the wall. There was a scruffy bearded white boy who towered over 6 feet tall. The other kid was some short scrawny Spanish kid. To break the ice I joked saying *those initials on the wall are missing the last S.*

I probably should have kept my mouth shut because only the white kid laughed. A.S. was the other person in the cell. He was proud of it being there, as a sign that he'd been here before. He said he'd let my comment go and chalk it up to a rookie mistake.

That's when I first learned there are two types of people in jail. The ones that thrive on it as a sense of pride and seem to always want to get back in. The other half are just looking for a way and to stay out.

A.S. was released later that afternoon. So it was just me and Lenny from *Mice & Men*. Before I knew it we were summoned to the paddy wagon. I was about to be escorted to jail.

Inside the sheriff van, the guards asked us if we wanted to listen to any music. I remember saying to myself. Wow, what nice people. They only extended that act of kindness because they knew we were all up shit's creek.

I was so worn out from the day that I was pretty calm on the ride over to jail, surprisingly. As we passed a gas station. *I took note of the price of* *gas being $1.95 gallon and a pack of Newport's having a $5.15 price tag.* I exclaimed,

"Damn, shit's expensive over here."

Why I gave a shit about gas and cigarettes at that very moment I have no idea. Two minutes later, we arrived. The barbed-wired, electrically charged gate crept open. As we drove through, the guy behind the wheel put his arm on the seat next to him, tilted his head and said,

"Good Luck Boys."

Just like that, the cattle doors sprung open and the herd was sent to slaughter.

CHAPTER 9

Barking Dogs

I don't know if you've ever been to a dog park. But when a new dog comes to the park for the first time, the other dogs usually all gather around to check out the "new guy."

The first time I ever took my dog to one of those parks, he was timid of the other canines. As soon as my dog entered into the other dog's domain, they went nuts, running towards him, barking and circling him. Trying to size my dog up, they made their presence known.

I had a big dog too--a Rhodesian Ridgeback. He was left shaking and terrified for fear of being attacked. Out of the pack emerged some little punkie runt. It lifted its leg and proceeded to piss all over my dog's face. Once the runt was finished, the pack disbanded and continued with its daily routine. That's kind of what jail is like.

Jail still felt so surreal and more like a bad dream than my present reality. At that point, my biggest concern was not letting the other "intakes" see my penis while we were forced to undress and go through cavity searches with the guards. After they are positive that you aren't clenching anything between your butt cheeks or have vials of crack rock under your tongue, they hand you a dark blue jumpsuit. It felt like the outside of a pair of Dickies throughout the outfit and smelled as if it had been dragged through the rain by a wet dog.

You are given matching dark blue t-shirt and shorts that feel more like sandpaper than cotton. Finally the new threads are topped off with slide-in, puke orange slippers. They are called "BoBo's" on the street.

There is no easy way to put this. It is degrading to have to squat naked in front of an officer and spread your ass cheeks. Having someone's finger in your asshole checking for drugs is one of the most sickening feelings there is. I was beginning to feel the effects of this enormous culture shock.

It was around 5pm. Everyone was in the mess hall eating dinner. I was escorted in with my hands behind my back, made to walk one foot over the other. Once the inmates took notice of me, their synchronized harmonic chewing and drinking came to a dead stop.

They all turned to take a look at the new catch that landed in their boat. Like the dogs in that park sizing up their competition. Still caught up in the hysteria of it all, being forced to detach from mainstream society into what seemed like a black market type of underworld filled with its own rules and regulations, I needed to seek refuge from the intense glaring looks I was being thrown and took a seat at a table with only one kid at it. A young looking Peruvian that didn't look a day past fourteen. He introduced himself as James.

Trying to get my bearing, I leaned in to ask him a question. Before I could connect my syllables to make a word an officer rang out.

"NO TALKING DURING MEAL"

A tray of slop was slid in front of me and I was given two pieces of bread. Not being hungry, I spent the rest of the meal just sitting there. Staring aimlessly. James signaled for my white bread, gesturing if he could have it. I nodded my head in compliance then watched this boy meticulously rip off the crust. Like a child would ask his mother to do while making his lunch for school. *What a child,* I thought.

Before I knew it, we were ordered into the day room where we were allowed to quietly talk, play cards, and watch TV on chairs bolted to the ground. The room had oversized bulletproof glass windows that let you peer out and witness freedom.

I felt my body change into survival mode, operating on adrenaline and sheer panic. I began to dissect time, challenging myself to persevere through every second, not thinking of time as a surplus of luxury, but of dwindling moments. I used James as my point of comfort upon entering the mess hall and pursued that option again as I pulled up a seat next to him in the day room.

He was at the table with two other cronies, Lewis, who was a Jamaican immigrant that couldn't stay out of trouble. He looked like a hybrid of Don King and Ruben Studdard. He had a certain charm to him, I must admit. He also had "Killa" tattooed across his stomach.

The other kid, Wiggins, was from a neighboring inner city county. Suburban towns take in inmates from surrounding cities to help control over-crowding, in return that county receives state money, or "aid."

He was in here for selling crack and aggravated assault with a deadly weapon. Someone owed him money so he drove by in his friends SUV. He hung out of the back window and clocked the kid in the head with a Louisville Slugger. In Wiggins' own words, he said *"I Barry Bonds' that nigga."*

The only time something exciting happened was when a fight broke out or a new inmate was being processed. It was like a bad Alcoholic Anonymous meeting. "Hi my name is ... I'm here for committing.... And have this long of a sentence."

Everyone knew when they would be released and treated that day like their new birthday. James asked me the usual who, what, when, where, and why, and I told him flat out I was here for a robbery charge and had 90 days, unless I got acceptance into rehab first. I concluded my introduction with **"I have no idea when I get to go home, how 'bout you?"**

Basically skirting the question with a less than amusing response of,

"Yea same shit, I'm still awaiting trial."

Not wanting to push my boundaries and test the waters, I left it alone, killing time on the couch until our lock down at 7:30pm. The previous night I was sleeping in my own bed, under my warm sheets, laying on top of my comfortable kings down mattress my parents had bought me. Now I was resting on a gym mat placed atop a plastic box spring, a bag filled with sand as my pillow, and a 1970's ratty looking crochet blanket used to keep warm. My decorated bedroom walls were replaced by stark white, industrial grade cinderblocks, my furniture consisting of a connected steel water fountain and toilet. A thick, green cold metal door sealed me in. The last sounds you would hear at night were the old rusty gears turning as the guards key locked you in.

In May, the sun is still up at 7:30pm. I would have just been eating dinner with my parents. Instead, I was locked down and forced to go to bed. What a difference a day makes.

My juvenile detention center modeled itself after a military institution.

They enforced strict structure with an important attention to details and rules. It is a lot to take in, so they assign you a "buddy" to show you the ropes. My buddy was James. He had been there ten months already and knew the conformity of this place like the back of his hand. He taught me how to make my bed with hospital corners. The sheets had to be so tight that if need be a quarter could bounce off it. Same went for your clothes. They had to be rolled a certain way so that it was easier for the guards to check for contraband. James outlined the do's and don'ts of this hell hole for me.

My first full day there, I felt like I was going to die. Waking up in that place opened my eyes to what my life had become--a cell number. Lucas Mancini was replaced by Cell 84.

I woke up in a cold sweat, dizzy and nauseous. In the morning, I had to shower, which consisted of being locked in a tiny room with a nozzle that dispensed cold warm water. You were given a hotel soap bar and shampoo packet. You had minutes to get naked, get clean, and get dressed. Believe me when I tell you that door would spring open no matter how far along you were in the cleaning process. Five minutes meant five minutes and not a second more.

James gave me the pro tip of not letting my feet touch the ground while in the shower because of all the pee and cum stains that had built up over the years. Every day, I was doing a balancing act trying to keep my feet in my slippers while not letting any of my clothes touch any part of the room. Sadly, I was always a clumsy motherfucker.

I had only been here a day and already this place was kicking my ass. Solitude and confinement wreaked havoc on who I was. I quickly learned, I was not made for this.

The funny part about juvie, is they have school. You have actual classes like math and history but they are taught in a very different way. It's more of babysitting criminals while asking them 1 + 1 or who the first president was than hardcore learning. Pencils and textbooks are dangerous, so we didn't get those either. Also, there was no cutting class, but I think that goes without saying.

I was trying to be forgotten and blend in as hard as I could. The thing is I was still the new guy. And everybody remembers the new guy until another new guy walks through those doors. What I did next though didn't help my chances of fitting in.

Sitting in school, right before lunch break, I was overcome with the sudden urge to vomit. I didn't know the proper protocol for this. All I knew is if I opened my mouth, projectiles were coming out. So I made a break towards the trash can. As I bolted for the trash, I saw Officer Mames step in front of me.

Before he could finish his sentence of *"What the fuck are you do..."*I splashed about two gallons of puke on him and fainted. I didn't have time to feel embarrassment until sixteen hours later when I woke up in my cell.

Having to come out of my cell for the first time after throwing up on an officer was almost as worse a feeling than the one I got coming to jail. I was terrified that my life was about to be made a living hell by everyone especially by my fellow flunkies. I thought it was a real bitch move and figured they would think the same.

To my dismay, this wasn't the case in fact, it was the total opposite. The officer I threw up on was the most hated guard there. He would belittle the inmates during cavity searches, violate us during shake downs by yanking our shorts up to our chests, leaving our balls in our stomachs, and regularly deny phone calls home. Mames was a total prick.

A fact that was explained to me by James. I did, what every person locked up there had ever wanted to do, sort of, besides beating the hell out of the guy. Throwing up on him was a close second.

Years later, I would regularly run into Officer Mames at a popular Diner called Rosie's. He never actually recognized me, but I swear he knew who I was. After lunch one day, my then girlfriend and I were walking past his table to leave. His chair was sticking out so I knew I wouldn't be able to get past without saying excuse me. I decided to do the more mature thing and pretended to throw up. Mancini 2, Mames 0.

The first Mames throw up incident got me in the good graces of my fellow felons. James and I were becoming real friends. What started off with sitting at his dinner table watching a little kid take off the crust to his sandwich evolved to him helping me pass daily roll call and letting me view the pictures girls had sent him saying they how much they missed him.

We developed a friendship, a common bond. I can't say I was proud of it, but it felt comforting to be able to lean on someone in such a foreign situation for me.

I still didn't truly know why James was here though. He said same as me, but he had already been here ten months, without seeing a trial. That's illegal in the juvenile court system in the state of New Jersey.

Something wasn't adding up, but I didn't have the balls to ask him until one afternoon in the rec room. He was sitting across from me playing spades. I leaned in, a bit of hesitation in my voice I lowered to a grumbling tenor pitch, before uttering out

"James, why are you here dude? Ten months, still awaiting trial, for the same crime as me? Just tell me, don't bullshit, I don't judge, that's what God's for."

I could tell I caught him off guard. A long pause followed.

"Murder."

Now I was the one caught off guard. Fishing around in my brain for the correct response, James took the lead.

"I'll tell you if you want, it isn't like we got somewhere to be"

I nodded yes. I couldn't help but feel compelled to hear this.

"Have you ever beaten anyone to unconsciousness?" He asked.

I shuddered the word no.

You have no idea about the power you feel then when you are that in control. A switch of viciousness goes off. Then there is no turning back. I'm not some brutal thug. I'm not proud of what happened. I just couldn't stop it. The papers call me a savage. I'm not a monster. I killed Amber Mason when I was 14 with a knife and my bare hands. I love my brother.

I was about to get a firsthand account of a bloody senseless murder from the one who did the killing. I didn't know if it was legal for him to share this with me or morally right to hear this but I couldn't stop listening. My eyes were glued on James. I motioned my facial expressions to say keep going.

My brother always hung out with this chick. I was sleeping upstairs when he came running in saying he needed my help in the basement. When I got downstairs I saw this bitch nearly knocked out bleeding from her head. My brother said she tried to kiss him and he hit her. Shit got real when she threatened to go to the cops. That's when we both beat her until she wasn't moving. I got a knife and we went to work.

"Went to work?" I asked.

I stabbed her in the throat. Her eyes popped out and began to bleed. She wasn't fully dead yet. I had to cut off her head to make the noises stop. There was so much blood. Me and my brother must have thrown up about 3 times each because of the smell.

The smell?

Oh man, the smell of blood and guts is fucking disgusting.

I should have just stopped him right there. There was no need for me to hear this, but I blurted out. "What did you do with the body?" instead.

That's where shit started to get fucked up. She was kind of fat and it was all dead weight now. We sawed off her arms and legs, and stuffed them into garbage bags. We had to put the pieces in a steamer trunk because of the odor.

"You left the body in your basement?"

No… let me finish. By the time everything was cleaned up it was like 4 am. My cousin's quinceanera was only a few hours away so we decided to go to sleep and dispose of it later that night when we got back.

I told my brother to just have us do it, but we needed somebody to drive us.

"Drive you where?" I exclaimed.

To dump the body in the Passaic river.

Did you?

NO. Right when we pulled over to lift the trunk out of the car, two cop cars rolled up with their guns drawn.

DROP THE TRUNK they said. When we did, the top flew open and her head rolled out.

"Then what happened?" I said.

This happened. They want to give my brother the death penalty. I'm going to get life in prison.

That was the end of story time as a few other cellies sat down to play cards. I thought after hearing all that it would change my opinion about James. Think that story did more for my ego than anything else. I felt like I had the biggest, baddest mother fucker in this place on my side.

I had been there so long I had made it to the top tier, the "gold" level. I was allowed a radio with headphones, given an extra phone call, and a later bed time. I had more time to interact with the staff and shoot the shit with the other "privileged" cellies.

It was mostly just me and James though because the other kids were too wild and untamed yet to follow the rules set forth by the establishment. The time he spoke about the murder was the last time either of us had brought it up. I was having an escaping experience forming a bond with someone that had it worse than me. It gave me hope in myself.

I knew James was at a crucial point in his life. He was about to go on trial for his case, over a year had passed with him waiting in juvie. He was about to be transferred to an adult jail at the age of sixteen.

We both shared the coveted gold status which entitled us to ten minutes of computer time on Wednesday. I personally didn't care because they blocked all the sites I wanted to see, MySpace, instant messenger, etc. My family also visited me on a regular basis and constantly wrote to me so I was always in touch with the outside world, but for James it was a different story.

Wednesday night computer night was his only time to learn about the world. His eyes glued to the screen while he surfed the net. The only caveat being James wasn't allowed to Google search his case. So he made me do it for him. The results that came back read like a horror show; countless articles with headlines describing the attack as heinous, savage, and brutal. The press panned the brothers as monsters and devils.

James sat back in his chair. Motionless, he had an empty look in his eye. I wasn't about to say anything. The situation spoke for itself. James bit into his pound cake and took a sip of milk before whispering,

"Thank God Pastor Dan comes tomorrow."

Before I could ask him who Pastor Dan was our ten minutes were up and we were whisked off into lockdown for the night.

CHAPTER 10

The Shepherd & The Sheep

Once and awhile at Juvenile Detention, they would have special guests or groups such as a bible class or an army recruiter come in. On this day, it was a gentleman by the name of Pastor Dan Delorenzo, Chaplin of Morris County. Normally I would just opt to play cards instead, but James had mentioned him the previous night so I figured I would try this one out, what did I have to lose?

At first glance through the big windows in the dayroom, I mistook Pastor Dan for my Uncle Brooke. I remember thinking, "Why's my Uncle here?"

In reality, he looked nothing like my uncle, but from afar they had a striking resemblance due to their olive Italian skin, white puffy almost pompadour hair, tailored sport jacket, and fitted sweaters. They both wore classy watches and when I finally met the Chaplin, I noticed the trademark cologne. Even through the bullet proof glass, I could feel the warmth of this man's heart.

I had already been there twenty days and like I mentioned before was getting a little too comfortable and accepting of my situation, as opposed to my initial mission of soul searching, weeding out the root of my problems.

I walked into the room with Pastor Dan with "jail swag" I'll call it. The type of walk that someone does that tries to exude confidence but in fact is covering for their shortcomings. I sat down, in the back, about five other inmates, including James were there. Pastor Dan spoke with a soothing tenor like voice, always changing his pitch to emphasize the importance of what he was saying. Occasionally bringing it down to a near whisper, with a stern undertone triggering goose bumps on your body, his eyes filled with identification and compassion to your cause. Something inside me told me to trust this man.

He never pushed religion and ritual on you, opting to help lost souls find their own spirituality and understanding of God. That is what drew me to him. He wasn't a preacher, but a helper to mankind. He was the shepherd for the sheep of troubled youth.

Pastor Dan spoke for thirty five minutes about pain and how we must forgive, learning to appreciate all aspects of life, no matter how big or small. Whether you're lucky enough for a butterfly to land on a branch next to you so you can admire its beauty or are afforded an opportunity you otherwise wouldn't have, appreciate it. Love what you have, and not what you want.

Each time he opened his mouth, he struck another cord in my heart, I was finding hope and encouragement in his words, putting me in a meditative state of mind, relaxing my senses.

Lowering my defenses wanting to be found, I began to weep softly. Not wanting to draw anyone's attention, I put my hands in a V shape over my nose and mouth. Using my fingers to try and block to onslaught of waterworks that I felt coming on.

My lip quivered, I bit down hard with my front teeth, struggling to keep my composure. Every sentence this man said was ripping at my heart. By the time he was done speaking, I had pulled myself together, not without Pastor Dan taking notice though.

Everyone cleared the room to return back to daily routine, as I was leaving Pastor Dan put his hand on my shoulder, turning me around he could still see the residue of cries left behind. Gripping his hand around the back of my neck, laying his forearm on my shoulder, lowering his voice to a raspy mellow tone he told me:

"I know you hurt kid, and I know you have a long journey ahead of you, I can help you, I'll be there every step of the way if you and your parents let me, I have to go, but we'll be in touch."

The next week and half went by just like the previous twenty one days did, slow. Still entrenched in the routine of 6 am wake ups, five minute cold showers, and food you probably wouldn't even feed your dog. I was growing more desperate to feel the comforts of home.

Pastor Dan got the wheels spinning in my head and after mentioning him to my parents we all thought it would be a great idea for him to accompany me on this escapade.

I was growing restless, not knowing when I was going to be able to leave juvie for rehab, wondering what it was going to be like, how long I was going to be there and what kind of strict regimen and rules they enforced.

My mind was racing. The fear of the unknown was getting to me. I wanted to get on with the next part of my life. All I wanted was to be one step closer to finishing this epic travel of mine. My mind was now past James and them and focused on getting MY life back.

I became increasingly frustrated, badgering my mom and dad with questions that they didn't have the answers to. Out of nowhere, my facility received a phone call in regards to an open bed at

Merseyside Village. What seemed to be at a standstill suddenly appeared to be full steam ahead and my anxiety of the unknown turned into the anticipation of a new beginning.

I was informed the next morning I would be leaving for Merseyside Village rehab and that my mother and father will meet me there with a suitcase of clothes and hygienic necessities.

I was ecstatic at first, being able to wear my own clothes again, using my own shampoo and soap, actual sneakers and not the BoBo's I had been wearing for the past month.

Full contact with my family during visits and an extra phone call a week had me beaming with confidence. It's funny how much you miss a hug from your mom when you suddenly can't have one.

The day of my departure from juvenile detention, I arranged a meeting with Pastor Dan to relay the details and gain reassurance from him that everything was going to be ok. I met with him and James ten minutes before lunch. We shared in prayer with one another, a blessing from God to help us on our separate journeys.

Five minutes after getting my tray and sitting down, the paddy wagon was here to take me to my next stop. A general disappointment originally swallowed the floor when everyone found out I was off to bigger and better things. It's always a somber moment when someone gets "out."

Partially because you feel bad you're still here and jealous they're not. Also, you develop bonds with these people you share such close quarters with. After the initial disappointment settled down, a surge of energy and cheers erupted. They were happy that I got to move on in the process and that I was no longer stuck lost in translation.

The guards let me high-five Wiggins, Lewis and them, and hug it out with James, unusual because there was a strict NO contact policy, but even the guards shook my hand and wished me well in my travels. I was then escorted into the intake slash processing room where my journey originally began, having to strip off freedom and don the robe of captivity. Now the roles were reversed and I got to enjoy shedding the cloak of lockup and embrace the tease of liberation, however brief.

I was still had handcuffs on my wrist and chains around my ankles with the rope around my waist making me look more like a beast than a human. But I didn't care. I still felt I had achieved victory.

I was about to leave detention when it was delayed five minutes because of an intake of a new prisoner. The iron clad door opens, hearing the rattling of a convict's chain, I look up and see A.S, the kid who carved his name into that holding cell and was released later that day, ended up coming here after all, just thirty days after we first met.

The last words that were said to me in juvie were, **"Don't come back."**

Trust me. I wasn't ever planning on it.

CHAPTER 11

HOTEL CALIFORNIA

Merseyside was a nineteenth century mansion converted into a therapeutic community. It was attached to a Coventry and surrounded by lush green gardens that were meticulously kept.

Pulling up, I saw my parents waiting for me on a wooden bench. My first impression of this new chapter was hope, change, and serenity. Unfortunately, those feelings didn't last long.

The first impression wore off quickly and before I knew it I had about twenty sets of eyes staring at me, the "new kid" syndrome people get. I remember thinking for as big as this place was, it sure seemed small when all these kids were cramped in there.

There must have been eighty kids or so in the place, of all sorts of backgrounds and history, each with something fundamentally wrong with them that led us to act violently or indulge in drug addicting behavior. All parts of Jersey were represented here, from the struggling black youth from Paterson getting high off PCP to the rich Valley girls of the suburbs smoking crack and snorting heroin. The foster children whose bad luck and misfortune had landed them next to kids whose grandparents' spoil the hell out of them with Rolexes and clothes. The washed up jock turned junkie sharing a room with introverted book worms, trailer park trash breaking bread with fist pumping Guido's.

The point I'm trying to make is this place was different, eclectic to say the least. It was like cruel **ALICE IN WONDERLAND** shock, falling through into a world of talking dogs, flying fish and inconceivable ceremonies. It was a sub culture of society where their law governed the land, and the Mad Hatter had complete and utter control. I felt like I was in a freak show, not because I felt I was better than these people, but all around me was chaos.

Crazy shit was everywhere. Young girls, screaming like banshees, pulling their hair out, starved for attention to my left. A boy no older than twelve in a shirt and tie, expediting orders to some nineteen year old slacker delegating him to wipe the baseboards and tuck in his shirt.

Ahead of me behind the front desk was an older male sitting stiff on an old, splintered, wooden church confession chair, with an expression of pain and discomfort taking siege on his body. As I walk down the long corridor into the admissions office, which was an empty room with an collapsible table and chair in it, two tough looking gentlemen with shaved heads, wearing boot cut jeans to complement their black converses and dark car heart jackets walked by, staring in intimidation at me until an administrator interrupted their concentration to introduce themselves to me.

The one was named Bill. He was going to be my "Big Brother," which meant that he would shadow me on my first stage of the program, Stage 6. Helping me adjust to life in that environment, answering any questions I might have.

The other one's name was Dave, he had a little Hitler mustache going on, but other than that, there's nothing more to write home about him. By the time I made it to the admissions room, my head was spinning, and I was petrified of this place already. I was more than ready at that point to turn around and rot away in juvie again.

I kept thinking "this will all be over soon, I'm almost home." I never put much thought into how long a stint in rehab for marijuana would be, after all, the only reason why I came here was to defer me from facing charges as an adult, since I was court ordered. So when James Trumbeani, the head administrator, sat down and opened his mouth and the phrase

"This is a 6-12 month program that you must complete in order to be released. Although you are court ordered here, the

door is open at any time and you are free to leave whenever you want."

When I heard that I felt my spirit was robbed. Like finding out you lost your job or that your significant other is cheating on you. It was a devastating blow.

The whole car ride to Merseyside Village, I had pictured my release. I started thinking about life again on that ride. I wanted to eat a fucking Big Mac or have a cup of coffee. I forgot what showering barefoot was like. And the next car I was in, I wanted to make sure the windows rolled down.

The taken for granted, daily amenities life, that's what I thought of. Now, I heard this? I caved, the two officers were still waiting there to make sure I stayed. I got up and told everyone I couldn't do this, I couldn't handle anymore. I was hell bent on going back to juvie, so what if I couldn't wear my own clothes and use the soap I wanted, I felt like I had just been dropped in the middle of P.T Barnum's circus. My panic was heard through the door and stirred a commotion within the hall. Now

I had these drug addicts trying to stare in and watch me.

I hate surprises, so when there unfavorable ones I usually flake out 99 percent of the time, it was no different here. In a moment of sheer selfishness, I had an epiphany in the sense that I stopped and took notice of the look on my mom's face. It was like an expression saying if you don't do this, and you break my heart again I'm going to die from a broken heart because of a lost son. I had to stay, at least try it out, if not to satisfy the courts and on my behalf, then for my mother, because what's the point of living life in selfishness, alienating the people you love the most?

I signed the paperwork, twenty minutes after I bid my family farewell, knowing I won't be able to see them for five weeks, the next "family day." I was now alone, in an unfamiliar place within an uncomfortable environment. All that was left was for me to join the *"freak show"* and start checking in at the "Hotel California."

Let me paint a more specific picture of this place.

As you walk in, there is a tall wooden desk, a makeshift concierge that operates as a switchboard that a resident sat on while fielding phone calls. Very professional looking, yet comical because usually sitting at that desk was a sixteen year old boy with a bowl shaped haircut in a mismatched dress shirt and pants with a funky old man's tie wrapped around his neck.

The walls were a hospital blue-ish green. The industrial carpet was a color of a cheap burgundy wine, giving off a funky odor of carpet fresh and sweat. Down the one hallway was the medical office where I remember hearing the moans of sick children, whether it is out of pain or conning deceit to get special privilege.

I was then taken on a tour by an elder tribesman I'll call him, with his shirt tucked in and pig Latin English, he said his name was Kyle, and before I could even think he took me along on never ending escapade through winding corridors, back breaking stair cases, and other quirky rooms that this evil house possessed. It was hard to keep up with him, snaking through the place I could feel my head spinning again. I knew I wasn't going to remember all this, just like when your boss shows you around the office and trains you on the procedures, it doesn't all stick at once.

All I wanted to do was go home, I didn't want to hear about how long I would be there, or even start to get acquainted with their rituals. I wanted to crawl up into a ball and go to sleep, or maybe throw up on Officer Mames again would help. I felt like a real bait and switch was pulled on me, like walking into the dealership expecting zero percent financing on the new car model and walking out with last year's closeout having to put money down and an interest rate of nine percent.

I thought this would be easier than juvie. A more natural environment, and better way to adjust and enter back into the "real world." It was told to me it was an honor and privilege to get a bed here, making it sound like I had just been accepted to Harvard or something. What kind of shit were they

145

trying to pull? After not being able to spot the sucker at the table, I realized I was the sucker.

Kyle didn't hold back one bit. He didn't even sugar coat it, instead talking about how he's completing the program in a month and how he can't wait to go home and get out of here. At one point in the tour, he told me he only volunteered to show me around because he didn't want to clean the house and be in group. He explained it to me. You sit on cold metal chairs in a circle and discuss various issues, whether it's a house meeting or encounter group, where every week you gather in a circle and "drop a slip," which is Merseyside lingo for writing the person's name on a piece of paper that pissed you off the most that week, put it in a lockbox and hope you get the chance to yell at that fucker, by the "guidelines" of course though.

Fuckin' crazy right? I use that language because that's what I thought, what the hell? Where am I? The major questions we ask about ourselves in our lives I was asking them all in about five minutes to Kyle. "Why do we do this?"

"How do I succeed in here?" and most importantly, "What do I got to do to get out of here?"

I was trying to learn more about what I would have to do to get out of here rather than learning the rules, but they go hand in hand, just like life, this place was a microcosm of the outside world.

Everything was inspected with a fine tooth comb Kyle told me as we entered the chapel. It was the most beautiful part of the house. This is where I found out this whole place was converted from an old church, and that there's a convent a mile down the road.

When Kyle mentioned it was haunted, I brushed it off thinking he was just trying to add to my woes. Ghost stories aside, the Chapel was architecturally inspiring. My first thought was 1930's French countryside. Then I quickly realized I was still in rehab.

Standing for a second, trying to capture a moment of serenity and take in the light echoing through the rainbow colored stained glass that had angels etched in it. The doors were heavy, cast iron and mahogany clamored for your eyes attention.

Sadly though that moment didn't last, as I was playing catch-up to Kyle who looped back around outside to the laundry room. Briefly opening the laundry room door, it looked like two malnourished child laborers slaving over tons of dirty clothes. We shut the door and continued onward, Kyle then informs me it's good to be on the laundry team because the laundry room is air conditioned and you can take what's in people's pockets, and sometimes their clothes if they give you too many for them to keep track of. That was good to know, I didn't send my clothes to the laundry room for a month after hearing that.

I wasn't liking Kyle too much, I mean the last thing anyone wants to hear that just entered a long term rehab is that YOU'RE completing in less than a month. And that this place is hell and good fucking luck. That was just a taste of the cruelty in this place. There is no love here I was finding out. Until me and Kyle made our way up the three flights of stairs that connected the basement to the third floor, which is where the male residents sleep.

Finally reaching the top, I was gassed, totally out of breath. Kyle opens this big white steel door that was the entrance to the third floor. As he's about to open the door he jokingly says,

"Welcome to the Inferno."

Immediately we were hit with a blast of heat and humidity that felt like we just opened a burning oven. There was no air conditioning in this place, and it was mid-June, and one of the hottest summers on record. Since heat rises, it has to go somewhere, and that somewhere was here, where we sleep.

When fifty or so guys share one floor, eight showers, six toilets, twelve sinks and its three guys to a room, it's going to smell. When it's hot, it's only going to smell more putrid, at least that was the case here. When I tell you that if you blended onions, spoiled milk, rotting eggs and a sweat rag and cooked it at 400 degrees, it still wouldn't stink as bad as this place did.

Kyle showed me where I would be sleeping, saying I'd get my bags later, and then opened the door to my room, where that smell was even more intense than in the hallway. This is where Kyle turns to me with gagging look on his face and says,

"Your rooming with Mochado, (with emphasis on the O to mock his name) that's a dirty motherfucker right there."

Then he shuts the door and opens the door to his room, which was across the hall. He motioned for me to come in. He sat on his bed, his room smelling very fresh and clean, like a new deodorant scent, he opened the top drawer to his dresser and took out two body building magazines.

"You know man, it's not that bad, you just got to follow the rules, and exert effort, keep your nose clean and make sure to talk about your 'issues."

Understanding the first part, I shot back a look of befuddlement,

"Issues?" I said, "What you mean?"

"Like the reasons you use drugs dude, I was a heroin addict, shootin' mad bags of dope everyday bro. I guess I was running from something and I came here and realized I couldn't live with myself. I was a closet homosexual. I let it out though man, everyone knows now. It took me getting high on a request and getting caught to realize it. Sitting on **"The Chair"** changed my life man. I finally breakdown and let the truth out. I'm not supposed to even have these male body building magazines, but I figured you'd want to look at them."

I first thought, **"Oh my god, he's hitting on me, in his room, on his bed, in a drug rehab."** My second thought was *"Wow, this kid has a lot more issues than being gay."*

I was undoubtedly freaked out. Since reformed Kyle wasn't allowed to have his 'dirty" magazines, he cut his losses realizing his fun was over and escorted me downstairs. Leaving me

151

sitting on a bench by the switchboard, I had about ten minutes I figured until I'd be whisked downstairs to be introduced to the rest of the troubled souls here. So I thought I'd use the time to just reflect and gather myself. I just kept thinking about my family, and home.

As a child growing up my dad would always take me to the batting cages, the arcade, or the occasional ball game. In his car while driving to these special places, we would always listen to Q 104.3, the Rock of New Jersey, and almost every time I would here the song "Hotel California" by the Eagles, and I absolutely loved it.

Being an enthusiastic nine year old, I was more hooked on the beat and mellow hymns, than the actual lyrical content. It's funny and sadly ironic because if I had only listened to the words of that song, it would have foreshadowed where I would have ended up. "Hotel California" is a slang term for a lifetime drug rehab facility in California, called Synanon. Serious drug addicts that had very little shot of ever living a productive life in normal society would seek refuge there. In the song, The

Eagles map out what Synanon was all about claiming,

"This could be Heaven or this could be hell...I called up the captain to bring me my wine, we haven't had that spirit here, since 1969... Mirrors on the ceiling, pink champagne on ice, we are all just prisoners here from our own device, in the masters chambers they gather for a feast, they stab it with their steely knives, but just can't kill the beast. Last thing I remember, I was running for the door to find the place I was before, "Relax" said the night man, we are programmed to receive, you can check out any time you like, but you can never leave." – Hotel California (paraphrased)

Synanon was a place founded on military principal with intense structure and rule programming that's sole purpose was to break a person down so they were reassembled with those morals set forth by that establishment, aka brainwashing.

The concept is called "therapeutic community," but trust me, there is nothing therapeutic or tranquil about it. It's called that because from day one, their mission is to pry open the closet of hurt and dysfunction in your heart. Sometimes using it in manipulative tactics against you to open up and confront your issues, from the inside out. They treat drug addiction as a symptom, which I agree is a valid argument, but the way about treating the symptoms is what I call into question. It is in this strategy and technique of tearing a man down to slowly program him back up the "right way" that Merseyside was founded on. A direct offspring to Synanon, the only difference being, Merseyside didn't keep you there for life.

Over the course of the next few weeks and months, I would learn the inner workings of this almost underground and definitely hidden way of life. Undertaking their ritualistic practices, learning the language they used, and abiding by outrageous rules that seemed more like commandments than guidelines. I of course, got to know the people I labeled "freaks."

I was now about to enter the jungle. I was told by an administrator to go downstairs. I was about to join the "family."

CHAPTER 12

Helloooooo Family.

"SEEEAAATTTTTSSSS!"

A single howl is let out throughout the house, followed by several roars repeating the same word. A stampede of kids comes running from all directions to gather in the main dining room, snapping up chairs from the perfectly distanced tables and twist them around facing the front "clock," the time hanging on the wall in front of the eating quarters.

Everyone orderly filed, lined up on the fouth tile from the wall, three tiles in between chairs, sitting upright, feet flat and spaced, arms at your side, in utter silence, very cultish. Me, being the new guy didn't have a damn clue about what was going on. My "big brother" I told you about before, Bill, yeah, well, he was nowhere to be found. Through the law of observation I took my seat and tried to blend in. Although as I looked around, not everyone was taking their seats as told, instead straggling around, or at the tables lounging, singing R&B melodies, clowning around.

A blonde haired, slightly tanned girl cries out to the mob of reckless souls,

"People! *STOP 'DOPE FEINING'* get in your seats. We have Caseload next!"

"SHUT UP! Lauren, no one wants to hear your mouth, go throw up again."

"Heeey, Antonio, that's not nice,"

All of a sudden a goofy man with oval shaped glasses complimenting his head, pops up out of nowhere, swaying his fat hips while he walks, rolling his wrist with his pointer finger out, talking in a whimsical sarcasm, lowly pitching his voice

"*Antonio, line up outside the coordinators office. Now!*

Everyone else, get the fuck in your seats, *don't you want Caseload? If not, well cut that too and make you scrub and G.I the house again.*"

"What the fuck is going on?" that's what I thought, I started the day in a jailhouse cell. Sitting around playing cards all day, yapping about dumb shit, four hours later, I'm in a place that better resembles a Jim Jones worship center, than a drug rehab community. I later learned "dope feigning" is what Merseyside called slacking off. If someone reports a bad behavior of yours to the Coordinators office, whether it's something as small as your shirt not being tucked in or shoelaces not tied, to the very extreme like getting high, you get in trouble.

I told you they have strict rules, centered on tattle telling. Get in trouble enough times and you get "shot down," where they "freeze" your treatment and make you stay longer.

I knew none of that at this point though. I had just figured out what the hell seats were. It's

157

hard to keep track of eighty five criminals, drug addicts, and misguided youths in an unlocked facility. I had no idea why we were sitting, but we were. At this point, the first howl of seats was ten minutes ago, and just now did everyone finally sit down. It took another five minutes for the coordinators, or staff to approve the way all eighty or so of us was sitting.

Overwhelmed and shocked do not do justice to the feelings I had. Besides being scared in a new environment, with what seemed to be savages to me, I was flabbergasted at the language that was used. It was their own. The organization and humdrum of this place was relentless, structure and integrity met you at every corner. They were all being programmed to tell on each other, no secrets, or "guilt" they would say. I say being programmed because any variance from the establishment was against the rules, and there were many of those 'variances.' This is what I first noticed, partly because this information was given to me during intake, and the other part deciphered and pieced together by me through observation.

My head spinning worse than riding the most nauseating ride at Six Flags, I was scrambling to catch my bearings when a thundering voice rang out from the front of the room. It was one of the senior rehabbies calling order and taking role,

"ANDERSON, JENN"

"Here!"

"Athens, Kyle"

"HEREEEEE"

The "chief" cycled through the whole list of eighty plus patients, and I began to zone out. During this trance, I had a "eureka" moment, realizing the longer you're there and the better you do, the more "status" or responsibility you had improved your chances of quicker release, I immediately knew right then and there I had to keep my nose clean, adapt a different persona, and strive to be an unknown.

When all they want to do is to know and fix you that can be a tall order. I also told myself, don't associate or participate in any type of mischief and

159

learn and follow the rules as fast as possible. This was my only solid way to obtain freedom and earn my release from being "state property." It was a lot harder than it seemed to be, but I'll tell you now, I mostly stuck to that plan the whole way through Merseyside.

At the end of roll call, that same gawky man with the funny shaped glasses and wrist gestures from before appears before all of us. Standing straight in military like fashion, he greets us,

"Good Afternoon Family."

A ritualistic chant from the ocean of chairs shouts back.

"Good Afternoon RAYYYY!"

Ray continues.

"Alright, welllll before we break for Caseload, let's just take care of some quick business, we have two new intakes today, they're here, if Chris G, and Lucas M can stand up and greet the family. Start by saying "good" followed by the time of day, morning, afternoon, or evening, and address everyone as family. Then if you

can just tell us a little bit about yourself, where you're from, what brought you here, and your drug of choice, k? Thanks."

Resistant to change, I was not quick to stand up and break my comfort zone. I found nestled along a nook in the wall. Chris G went first, understanding he wouldn't talk forever I prepared myself for my big introduction. I never shied away from a crowd or a public speaking opportunity but this was a little different. It felt like it took me all my energy to get out of that chair, feeling like 500 pounds of meat, I picked myself up, knees and hands shaking the whole time, I cleared my throat, as I began to speak my voice cracked

"Good Afternoon Family.'

"Good Afternoon Lucas."

Moans back at me.

"I'm 17, from a town not too far from here in Chelten County, I came from Juvie, and my drug of choice is Marijuana."

I sat down and felt like I had just officially dropped off the face of the earth. I was nowhere on the map of society or relevance. It was a very lonely feeling, being left to heal and find solace in the lonely people that are coming to you for help. People helping people in similar situations are only healthy and effective if those people are adequately equipped with the right mental attitude and capacity to assist one another is how I feel.

With that being said, I was in the worst state of mind I had ever experienced. Total despair, with no hope because I had no clear vision of when this would all come to an end and just stop. I was afraid of tomorrow. It was the fear of the unknown.

For the rest of the day I tried my best to blend in, I wandered around that place in misery, the building and grounds were visually gorgeous but the energy and spirit inside was drudgery with failure permeating within the halls. Towards the end of the night, with the long day finally coming to a close, we were all disbanded into clean up duty after our nightly 8pm snack, which consisted of a peach cup or granola bar by the way.

I avoided Kyle the whole day after the episode earlier, and didn't find a single soul I wanted to associate with until I stumbled across an older looking guy, I pegged him to be at least twenty four, and since this was a rehab for minors I figured he was staff. He had a broom in his hand though and was pretending to sweep, minding his own business and looking humbled, I decided to probe him with a few questions. I don't know what made me approach him, he had kind blue eyes, but had a blank stare to them, like those crystal blues wanted to shatter and repent all their sin. After a brief exchange, I learned he wasn't any part of staff.

He was a twenty one year old who was deeply tied up in the court system who was facing ten years in prison for charges ranging from heroin and burglary to gun possession and credit card fraud. That confirmed my feelings and I was ready to walk away and continue to be lost in the shuffle of time until he mentioned he had been here before. The only reason why he was is back was because he wrote Merseyside a letter a day for five months while in jail. Like Andy in *The Shawshank Redemption* writing the governor for library funds.

They did this kid a favor and let him come back, even though he was an adult. He also mentioned to me that he knew this place inside and out and that he could help me get out quicker since he was adept to this environment and after hearing my story. He agreed to help.

I knew I could use him to my advantage, I stuck out my hand as sign of friendship and simply stated,

"I'm Lucas bro, nice to meet you,"

"Yea man, I'm Ron, Ron Duster, **I'll take care of you dude**."

I never thought a twenty one year old heroin addict who's a complete stranger would bring me such comfort and reassurance. Those words meant everything to me. It was the closest thing to the chapel I had felt and I don't know why but I didn't view Ron as the rest of these people. Maybe because he came off more mature and street wise than the others, I experienced sympathy towards him. Hanging on his words, holding them to a higher meaning, I still didn't know why, but I was drawn to him.

It's funny how you are made aware of your own ignorance sometimes. After me and Ron's discussion it was time to go off the floor and go to sleep. It was 10 pm we had an hour before lights out were implemented, I was worried about finding my luggage and belongings my first night, rather than showering and brushing my teeth, and since Kyle told me my roommate was a dirtball, hygiene wasn't a priority that night.

In the midst of all the chaos of change my stuff was misplaced and me and the other new kid, got our belongings switched. Before I put two and two together, I unzipped his luggage and started unpacking his things into my area I shared with two other patients. As I was sorting through everything I began to notice irregularities.

Knock off dollar store brand shampoo and shave cream, rough unscented soaps, along with wrinkled and tattered clothes. As soon as the thought of 'this isn't mine' entered my brain, the other new kid came into my room with my luggage.

With a look of embarrassment, he asked for his stuff back.

I didn't understand the justification of his body language until lights out, I was lying down on the top bunk, unable to sleep, and suffocating from the intense night heat and lack of air conditioning it hit me. The disappointment and anger I felt from seeing the "cheap stuff" was his excitement and joy from having my things. Nice shampoo, dove soap, name brand clothes. Only then realizing it wasn't his and had to trade it back to his reality. I think that's when I started to become conscious of how grateful I really should be, then walked in Machado.

This grown child was no taller than **4 ft. 9** and had a slight hunchback. Unkempt, *overly greasy hair*, his glasses taped together, **he looked like a mole, or rat**.

This mole rat was sleazy too, barging into the room hoarding snacks and stuff he stole from the kitchen hours earlier and had hid during the day. His grimy yellow sweat stained socks dragged on the floor, passing an odor throughout the room. He was eighteen but looked fourteen, had a beak for a nose, and a total disregard for authority and anyone's stuff but his.

He would pick his nose than eat a cracker with the same fingers, touching his face after, probably contributing to his severe acne. I tried to be nice to him but all he told me was that he loved crack rock and enjoyed smoking it, and to not touch his stuff. I told him to take a bath, he flipped me the bird then started picking the crud from toes and shoving cookies in his mouth. That's when my third roommate, Keith came in, luckily in the nick of time because I was ready to throw up from Mochado's grossness.

A complete contrast to Mochado, he came in freshly showered and shaved, a blue towel dangled from his neck. He was like a ghetto white kid, but had a lisp so he couldn't be scary or intimidating, because once he opened his mouth it evened out his hard ass persona.

In fact I found out he really wanted to get clean, he was smoking PCP every day, and that shit makes your brain bleed, so he had killed too many brain cells already, and since he wasn't born with many, he sincerely wanted a second chance.

He controlled Mochado, Keith towered over Mochado too. They made an interesting pairing, like Lenny and George from *Of Mice and Men*. Keith, who followed the rules to a T, never getting in trouble, and Mochado the crack smoking misfit who steals and lies any chance he can get. Plus he doesn't shower.

Before I knew it, time had passed and it was 11pm, lights were going off in a matter of seconds. I climbed into my top bunk and laid on the hardest mattress I had ever felt, worse than the sand mats in juvie. What made it worse was the heat and smell. Just lying there I would pour out sweat, the sheets were starched to the extreme, extra stiff, and we all had a fire blanket, which helps cover your body in case of a fire. Mine hadn't seen a washing room in years, stinking of moth balls and the wood from the back of a cob webbed closet.

It made my skin itch and only added to the discomfort. Making my body feel like it was stuck in hot syrup. Unable to move freely and making my sweat stick to my body I felt like I was in a strait jacket in what Kyle described best as "an Inferno." I passed out that night having my last few thoughts, the day flashing before my eyes. From waking up behind bars, to tasting fresh air for the first time in a while, transitioning into a house full of drug addicts and bizarre rule following, Kyle's sexual advance, Mochado, and everything in between. I was exhausted.

I'm not going to lie the next few days were rough for me, just like in juvie. On the third full day I was there, it was 7:30 am and we just finished our daily morning meeting, where we would recap events, convey announcements and appointments, along with giving affirmations to your peers, all while sitting on unforgivingly cold and hard metal chairs, stiff as a nail the whole time.

I lost my equilibrium and marched upstairs to the administrator's office where James

Trumbeani was and demanded I go home, or at least be taken back to my previous institution.

Citing their open door policy, being free to leave any time, I put up dignified front for about an hour, until they broke my front lines, and flanked both sides by calling my parents. Feeding me threating lies telling me how I'm going to go to Jamesburg, which is an adolescent prison in New Jersey, for three years, and it's in my best interest to stay. I caved, eventually integrating myself back into "the family."

I had this battle with myself every day, whether to stay or go, always feeling like I was fighting a lost cause. Not being able to make sense of any of it and being able to adjust properly, I wasn't allowing myself to pick up the pieces and continue on my way to a normal teenage life. Whatever was left of it at least.

This inner struggle went on for a solid two weeks after my attempt to split on day three. It only began to subside when I found out Pastor Dan was coming to visit me. My parents contacted him and set it up with Merseyside Village. I was there for about three weeks when I finally got to see Pastor Dan, it was the biggest relief. It was like peeing after a long car ride, relief. We sat on benches by a butterfly bush, hearing his voice was soothing to my ears, his cologne once again triggering a relaxing response to my senses. Finding comfort in his poetic rhetoric, like a cup of soup on a frigid winter night, it warmed me up. It felt good to talk to someone that understood my situation who didn't judge, and through conversation made any atmosphere seem tolerable.

We would talk about any and everything, from good Italian food to cars and watches in one breath. We would philosophize about life, people, and actions. Even the lowest form of intellectual conversation we had were special to me because for that brief time I would spend with Pastor Dan, he made me feel normal, in a very un-normal circumstance.

At the end of every visit, he would lean in, and put his hand around my neck, together we prayed. He would lead a prayer of hope and discovery. Asking for forgiveness and atoning for sin. In this kind hearted old Italian man's words I found inspiration to carry out and complete my journey. After every visit I would hang onto his words, clenching to them for rescue until our next encounter.

I went back to assume my duty within the "family" with a renewed sense of confidence and control, in a place that attempts any way possible to seize control, this is a huge advantage for one to have. I had self-assurance and guidance. Letting myself know every beginning has an end. Telling myself, when you stop trying to force a square peg into a round hole, everything just seems to fit that much better.

Thank you Pastor Dan.

Things started to go smoothly. I was fitting into the daily routine nicely, and was sticking to my mission statement of faking it until I make it. By playing the program, keeping my nose out of trouble, and participating in group sessions. Groups were usually sandwiched between eating and cleaning.

Ron and I had developed a bond, but it was all surface stuff, because even in a place where you are forced to be known, no one wants to be. It's a lot easier to shoot the shit with someone than taking a personal inventory and have a real introspective look at yourself. I was taking note of what to do and what not to do from Ron. The more I got to know him, the more his true colors showed. I was also finally off phase 6, which meant I no longer needed Big Brother Bill. He was basically absent through the whole "adjusting period."

Ron and Bill also forged a bond. I could tell it was much deeper than mine and Ron's. It didn't bother me because I started to look at Ron as more of a criminal and social deviant than a reliable, trustworthy friend. Their tag along was the man I spotted upon intake, Dave, the neo Nazi looking one with the Hitler 'stache, in the jeans and jacket. He was a funny kid, we interacted here and there only on the surface but, never in depth knowledge sharing.

Bill and Dave, seeing how I am acquainted with Ron, strike up a deeper friendship with me.

Hanging around them more often I was noticing how much hatred they had towards minorities. They shared a passion for enacting violence towards everyone in Merseyside Village that wasn't pure white, they deeming being Jewish not pure white. It was only then, when their racism and bigotry was so prevalent and exposed around me did they ask me to join their mock white supremacy group.

"The Whites of Hell."

Since the group is made up of about seven members, all of which being heroin addicts and gun toting felons. I told them I had to think about it, and would get back to them. I'm not racist, nor do I ever want to belong to any group or gang where individuality is taken away and replaced with conformity.

Luckily for me, the next day Bill was caught huffing cleaning supplies and was ordered to take a drug test, his results showing that he had ample amounts of heroin in his system. He had snuck the dope in between his belt and jeans. This explained why he was never around to help me. My big brother was getting high.

I laugh at that irony. I learned that out of all the bad behavior and rules there are, there are four you do not want to break. They are considered the Cardinal Rules of Merseyside Village. They are:

NO getting high.

No Sex, No Violence, and NO leaving the property (escaping).

Bill broke cardinal rule one, don't get high in rehab, for this, the rule is that you must expunge your conscious and "drop your guilt" which is the process of writing all your bad deeds in treatment on paper, and sitting on "the Chair." The thorny, middle ages looking priest wooden seat, where you must sit for 24 hours, no slouching, with only four hours to sleep, it can definitely be considered cruel and unusual punishment.

I had seen someone on it when I had walked in for the first time, and Kyle touched on it briefly during my tour, saying he sat on it and that's when he professed his "gayness." Once people realized they are literally screwed, they don't hold back and automatically become the whistle blower to all the other people's guilt they know and hold. Like when Kyle's back was against the wall and had to drop something big. Bill wasn't gay, so he opted for the rat everyone out route.

This creates a chain reaction and mass panic throughout the house, because even the squeakiest of clean politician has something to hide. As expected, Bill with nothing more to lose spills his guts on everything, including the Whites of Hell.

Indicating his coconspirators meant they all had to sit on the chair. I ended up avoiding ever answering their proposal. It was the end of my and Ron's friendship though, I had to finger point who I knew was in it. This didn't bother me because I had no true loyalty to these people, when push comes to shove. You have to look out for number one. I had a greater purpose than acquiring friendships and "guilt". I wanted to go home.

Ron wrote me off after that, maybe because his motives to befriend me wouldn't come to fruition, or he thought I was soft. Whatever the case may be, this left me alone and without anyone to talk to and interact with. I was forced out of my comfort zone to migrate and find a new way to keep my sanity. I was off phase 6, so I didn't need Ron to lean on anymore.

Since I was promoted to the next stage, I didn't have to hang around my fellow stage sixer's, which there were quite a few loco's in my group. I used to hate going to that group because there would always be two girls there crying and wanting to cut themselves, my first ever stage 6 group, this girl Rebecca stayed sobbing in the corner the whole time. She kept picking at her arm that was bandaged. The adhesive unraveled to expose deep cuts up and down her arm. She stabbed them with her nails, forcing them to bleed, she made me very uncomfortable. I never attempted to talk to her, flagging her as a true head case at the time. I think though I was afraid to know her because she was riddled with pain, and I just couldn't take any more of it, her being the most fragile of all of us, I thought it'd just be a good idea to stay away.

CHAPTER 13

D'Evils

I hadn't had a can of soda in over three months. I was sitting down reading a book during a rare leisure moment. The soda machine staring at me, enticing me to want one but having no money to buy one, like most of the people in there. In comes Lauren. The blonde haired, slightly tanned, green cat eyed Lauren. The girl I first saw trying to corral the herd of beasts into their seats. She had a sneaky look on her face, cautiously she whispered,

"I'm not allowed soda, but if I get one I'll split it with you if you don't say anything."

Nodding to her in compliance, she walked over with a cherry coke. I poured it into a glass and began to chug it. Only to abruptly stop half way through because of the incredible burning sensation

I had in my throat. Apparently soda burns if you're not used to drinking it. This clued me into how long I've really been out of touch with the main stream. As for Lauren, who wouldn't enjoy the company of a pretty faced green eyed girl?

We clicked instantly. We also connected on an emotional level. Feeding off one another's energy provided us with a little conversational oasis. Lauren was the first one to really know my past, and I let her in willingly.

My old high school counselor came by one day to drop off a yearbook that was given to me. Those pictures and memories from my life as a free man would have been of waste and no meaning if I didn't have Lauren to share it with. I had pictures to now go with my stories. I was able to let her into my thought process and past life. Letting her analyze me and dissect my raw emotions, I wanted her to know me, who I really was.

I had learned a few things about her too. The eating disorder she struggled with, the desire to be super model skinny, the ugly divorce of her parents and disconnect with her sister, leading her to develop a nasty coke habit. I viewed her as the female version of myself, suburban youth, given an abundance of opportunity, only to squander it away and end up here. She was my mirror, I felt she was my female duplicate, to a certain extent.

Lauren poured out compassion and empathy to everyone. Sometimes her kindness would undermine her. Accepting other people's intolerable behavior just to fit in and not make waves in the pool. Always offering a helping hand, she reached out to a lot of the people that I didn't dare talk to. I, having a closed mind at times, wrote a lot of these residents off as weak, ingrained in me from Markus during my days of cut loose. One of Laurens helping hands had reached out to Rebecca, the girl I stayed away from, the scab picker, Rebecca.

Lauren shed some light on Rebecca's situation to me. Helping me to understand her pain, and showing me why no one deserves to be ignored. She had a mother who was a prostitute, who would regularly bring home random men to sleep with, having sex in front of Rebecca because they lived in a trailer and space was limited.

She developed a heavy crystal meth addiction from being forced on the street at a young age to turn tricks so she and her mother could eat. Lauren told me, Rebecca would come in her room at night and ball her eyes out, crying for hours wanting to cut herself because that's the only way her pain would stop. Rebecca would say her blood represented the tears from her soul.

Lauren would constantly remind me of the hardships of others, at times calling me a baby for my lack of how to deal with the small stuff. All the while I thought she was trying to help me relate to the others, in hindsight, it was her teaching me empathy, showing me how grateful I should be, not taking things for granted, and accepting opportunities I had at my disposal.

As Lauren put it "you have no idea what you have butthead, don't be that person to find it after you lost it. Capture it before it goes away. No matter how bad it is, there's always someone that has it badder." I grinned, she spit out the same thing my father would always tell me, except in a different context and not articulated as well, but the underlying point was still there. Lauren showed me how lucky I was.

Her nickname for me was butthead, because I was always kicking myself in the ass with my-self sabotage. At times, there was no difference between my ass and my face.

The day I worked up the nerves and courage to finally ask Lauren what she thought of me, I was terrified. I sweated asking her because I had provided such a candid look into the window of my life I was terrified I vilified myself and painted the picture of a heartless bastard.

My favorite thing to do with Lauren was to open up my yearbooks and writings and show them to her. Talking about my life and how much I missed it. On this particular day we were doing just that, it was the day I was going to ask her how she felt about me, but every time I'd be ready to roll out the question, Rebecca would come and interrupt us, the first couple of times she was really happy, like a euphoric, cloud nine happy.

Another boy in the house liked her. Rebecca lacked any real social skills and came across gawky at times, so Lauren and I tried to coach her on how to play it cool and maximize the chance, but before we could make any headway, she'd dart off again trying to find her boy toy.

Lauren and I must have been interrupted three or four times, so before I could get interrupted again, I blurted out the question I stressed the answer to.

Before I could get Lauren to respond, Rebecca shot past us. Screaming her head off, Rebecca kept saying she wants to die. A total about face from five minutes ago when cupid's arrow shot her in the ass. Now she's trying to cuddle with death. Even under Laurens tutelage of compassion, I couldn't help but think. **"Wow, what a crazy bitch."**

Rebecca booked it, and runs off the property. My instincts took over, I felt compelled to chase her. I was frantically yelling for her to come back, Lauren right behind me, trying to help me track down Rebecca. Lauren ran track in high school and was naturally fast. Since I was forced to stop smoking I had a new found endurance. Lauren and I were able to catch up to Rebecca and restrain her.

Apparently the boy who liked her called her ugly, now for most people that'd roll off their back, for an emotional head case like Rebecca, it was like a monsoon had just wiped out her village. Once she was with us, we calmed her down and had her reassure us she was ok. Being borderline suicidal, we took what she said with a grain of salt.

Rebecca is now laughing at this point, almost psychotically, brushing us off, she walks back to Merseyside through the same path we just traveled. Lauren and I stayed in back of her, making sure she didn't turn and run away again. As we turn the corner of the trail, there is about an 8 ft. drop with a rope swing tied to a burly maple tree. Rebecca was in the middle of tying the rope around her neck and about to jump off the side of the ledge. I sprinted towards her but was unable to catch her before she jumped. I saw her body tighten up and her veins constrict, the color in her face turning from a light pink, to a deep red transitioning to a plumed purple. I caught her on the back swing of the sway of the rope, clinging onto her, Lauren grabs the rope, and we proceed to get the noose off from around her neck. We carried her back to the compound, she was alive.

Within ten minutes an ambulance came and whisked her away, first to a hospital, then to a mental ward.

Lauren and I were told by the staff to keep quiet about what happened, and that we did a noble thing. It was all going to be swept under the rug, being portrayed to the rest of the patients that Rebecca wanted to transfer to a facility that better suited her "needs". As we walked out of the office of the staffer on duty, Lauren gave me a big squeeze of a hug, and said

"I think you're an amazing person Lucas, I love that I have you to call my friend."

Dumb founded and taken back, I asked her where this was coming from.

"I answered your question silly, and promise me you will never let anyone's opinions vindicate your feelings, the only people that matter are the ones you let matter."

It was a difficult thing to process, timing is everything in life, and I don't know if that was the best timing for me to feel truly jubilated from Laurens response. What I did feel was exhilaration because for the first time in the longest time I can remember, I had a true friend, and a true friendship. Not founded on drugs, lies or ulterior motives, but through honesty, compassion and soul.

It is a refreshing and wholesome feeling knowing you are loved and liked because of who you are by someone who has no blood attachment to you, this may come easy to a majority of people, but this has been something that's evaded me for a while, the ability to make an honest friend. Lauren taught me a very valuable lesson, compassion. If it weren't for Lauren to take the time out to educate me, I probably would have let Rebecca just run. There would have never been a seed planted to help sprout the tree of compassion in my heart again. The first one died somewhere along the way. She helped me cultivate those lost feelings again, irrigating my soul to let the running waters of self-respect reach me.

It was great to make a friend, but I couldn't stop thinking about the politics of Merseyside Village. The wanting for everything to be out in the air and open, yet manipulate and control what enters into the general knowledge of the family, kind of like cable news TV. Regulating what is kept in a shroud of secrecy.

This was very off putting to me, and only added to my outlook of this place they call Merseyside. My saving grace this time was Family Saturday. Seven hours every eighth week, peoples' family were allowed to come and visit their kids. This felt like the night before your birthday, knowing tomorrow is your day you get to spend however you want. Being able to eat real food the mothers and fathers cook and bring in. You're treated to an abundance of sugar and sweets and an endless supply of soda. Oh, and family Saturday was your chance to re-up.

Re-up. As in, try to get as much illegal shit back into the facility as you possibly can. Although staff searches the grounds, rooms, and the patients high and low after family Saturday, that doesn't stop the kids from Merseyside from trying to sneak in cigarettes, alcohol, cell phones, and of course drugs. Trust me when I tell you, drug addicts are some of the craftiest, most innovative people going. With that being said, I'd say about sixty percent of all the contraband was never found.

I believe they only hold these events to show the parents what a happy, pleasant place this is. Image is everything to Merseyside, it controls their monetary pipeline. They need money and funding just like anybody else. Often times, family Saturday was our stage to the outside world, to showcase what great strides we've made, and how Merseyside was "working."

All the added privileges served as a bribe to the Merseysiders. So they're focused on the rare treats and goodies than spilling their guts to their family for them to go home. Ignoring to shed a light on all the fucked up shit that went on around here. We clearly belonged to a utopic cult like society.

Anyway, I got to forget about my hatred towards Merseyside for one day. Plus my mom was bringing her chicken parm and potato croquets, so I was what Charlie Sheen likes to call "Winning."

CHAPTER 14

That's All Folks

I am firm believer in the theory of time goes faster, and a lot easier when you have absolutely no distraction from family and friends. I feel being completely blocked off from the outside world is better than tasting society in sample sizes. Not able to have a full serving is very frustrating. That's why I believe Merseyside was harder than sitting in juvie. The constant reminder of normal life in your face, freedom to see loved ones dangled above you, making you reach greater leaps and bounds to access the rewards.

It was tough, and a lot of kids couldn't cut it, often opting to go back to rot in jail, or take their chances with the judge. That can also possibly explain why Merseyside had such a diverse crowd of residents, ranging from the naive, misguided pot head, to the criminally malicious. Violent drug addicts, reaching the peak of their heroin addiction, who were teetering on life or death, if they relapse one last time.

The turnover rate at Merseyside, whether because of someone's completion, choice to split, or administrative discharge, (fighting, constant drug use etc.) was relatively high, so garnering such an eclectic group wasn't that hard.

On this particular day, I was summoned by one of the residents with "status" to see my counselor because she had mail for me. Collette's office was right by the new intake station, where they take our picture and evaluation.

This day, I noticed quite a crowd gathering there. Apparently there were three new residents. The first of which looked like the Spanish version of Pauly Shore, with his loopy, almost Gerry Curl-esqe hair that portrays the image of a receding hairline. The sunken in eyes with the droopy bags under them, topped off with the mismatched 1990s wardrobe that puts Vanilla Ice to shame. The best part is that he must have still been hallucinating from whatever he took. He was screaming

"I'm mother fuckin' Jesus."

"*I saidddddd*, my name is Mother Fuckin' Jesus."

Before I could weigh in and throw in my two cents on Barrio brother Pauly Shore, the second of the three intakes turned to Jesus and shouted,

"Yeah? Well if he's Jesus, then I want to be Jesus too, call me Baby J."

My first thought of newbie number two was that he had some mental handicap. Half of me came to that decision from his baby Jesus comment. The other half of me noticed the way he looked. Close your eyes and picture a hairy Porky the Pig with a cleft palette. That was him to a tee, pink like a porkster too.

Before the situation became more enticing to watch, almost theater quality, Collette, my counselor, came out to seize order and reign in control. Collette loved control, and could be quite the authoritarian. She had the looks of a sexy college athlete, so if you're a guy, it would make you want to love her. But she was like more like that annoying tough older sister, who is uncomfortably manlier than you. Collette kind of made you fear and quiver when she was around.

Collette was also an excellent titty twister and professional ball buster, with that being said, I had now taken a seat in her office. After playing robo cop, Collette was now sitting across from me in her office decorated in cheesy softball memento and postcards of past residents, no real artistic flare.

Staring me down, the room filled with an awkward tension because I've been in Merseyside for about four months now and we'd never interacted outside of weekly group session. Even after Rebecca's failed suicide, she didn't really reach out. The discomfort of wanting my letters along with what this woman was going to tell me hit its climax inside me so I broke the awkwardness.

"What's with side show bob saying he's Jesus, and what's the deal with the other one? Is he retarded?"

Probably a little startled from how politically incorrect I came across, Collette uttered out a slight laugh and cracked a smile.

"Noooo Lucas, that kid isn't handicapped, his name is Billy and he's your new caseload brother, Billy is quite the character though, I'm going to need you to step up and take him under your wing, since you're becoming a role model within this community. Also, the other one who's going around saying, "Hi, my names Jesus, well the funny thing is, his name really is Jesus, he's Spanish. The third new intake, I don't know if you saw him, his names Brian and went to the same outpatient program as you."

Now that I knew I had to take porky the pig under my wing, Collette's comment about Brian didn't really stick, about him being in the same outpatient program as me. All I kept thinking was "Thaaa Thaaa Thaaa Thaaaaat's All Folks!

Collette kept the conversation going by giving me some letters. Two of which came from my one grandma, I used to call her City Nanny because she lived in Manhattan. The other one was dubbed Brooklyn Nanny, for obvious reason. City

Nanny had written me throughout my journey, I never received a letter from Brooklyn Nanny. A letter from my parents, and one from Jaimie. It was a thick envelope, and a little on the heavy side. I figured she wrote a short story and threw in a few pictures.

I had missed my Junior Prom, Memorial Day, Father's Day, and July 4th so far, along with Dan's birthday, and Seaside, which is where everyone goes to party after prom in Jersey. I was hoping this was an update on how things were at home, my heart wanted to know if all my friends missed me.

But to no prevail. Instead she told me how much longer I was expected to be here for.

At least another **7-8 months**.

Before I could say a god damn word, a slinky, Eminem blonde curly mop top, Slim Shady spin off caught my eye and yelled,

"Is that MOTHERFUCKIN LUKE MANCINI? I think it is, remember me? Its B-

Waters from IOP, fuckin' Brian Waters dude, what up?!"

His name echoed in my mind while I recalled who he was in my head, and then it dawned on me. This was the kid who was ninety days clean in my outpatient group, and had just been released from Jamesburg prison for fraud and theft charges. That one piece of information stuck out to me because he was the furthest thing from a predicate felon. He had manners, an appreciation for life and seemed to know the value of a man's freedom.

Brian was tall, way over six feet but couldn't put on a pound of fat to save his life. He had a wit to him. His sense of humor was cunning and made me laugh which is hard to do. He had a goofy hipster vibe to him, you could tell he was from off the beaten path and tried hard to fit into mainstream America, but every attempt at it he failed miserably.

He brought a constant energy with him, borderline hyper activity disorder, and I'm sure his coke problem didn't help him in that department either. Even with knowing his affinity for cocaine I actually believed in Brian and wished him success, trusting he would do so.

I didn't have hope for 98 percent of the people I met either locked up or in my immoral doings, but I did for Brian, seeing him in the same place as me though provided me a selfish comfort, and hope. Mostly because I didn't feel as lonely as 10 minutes ago before I saw him here, and I knew he wouldn't see daylight before me.

Our conversation was then interrupted by Billy, the new intake that was upstairs. This was my pet project from Collette.

My chance of talking about the eight month bomb she dropped on me was now gone as she shifted her attention to the evolving situation.

Billy walked outside, sat down on a picnic table and lit a Newport he had smuggled in. Obviously there's a no smoking policy in Merseyside, but people break that rule all the time, just not this blatantly. A crowd of residents gathered around, people shouting at him to stop smoking, using their technical terms to bolster their statuses amongst peers and supervision as morally responsible, even though they are guilty as shit.

As the staff arrived, they told Billy to stomp out the cigarette, performing their whole song and dance routine to try and get him to put it out, stopping short of physically taking it. Out of nowhere, Jesus, still tripping mind you, comes flying in, proclaiming,

"The power of Christ compels you to STOP SMOKING!"

Jesus then clocks Billy in the face with a right hook, knocking the cigarette from his mouth and Billy to the ground. Killing valuable brain cells the kid couldn't afford to lose. The staff pounces on Jesus, restraining him. Billy, slowly picks himself up. Dusting the dirt off his white sneakers, he proceeds to pick up his cigarette and take one last puff. With a bruise below his eye, he blows out a cloud of smoke and say's,

"Man. *Fuck you* Jesus."

CHAPTER 15

Bundles of Joy

They ended up packing Jesus' shit and shipping him off to some hardcore wilderness camp in Utah. Billy was able to stay after his first day shenanigans. He just had to sit his ass on the chair for 24 hours. I originally hoped they'd send them both off that way I wouldn't have to watch Porky's ass all the time. As much as I joked about Billy, I categorized him in the same class as Brian and Lauren. I sincerely wanted him to succeed and make it in life.

Billy introduced me and my family to his mother on family Saturday. Nina, Billy's mom was a sweetheart. Your typical larger, overbearing Italian mother who smothered her child with love and toys. Spoiling him from time to time, he was her baby. Her one and only child, she only wanted the best for her son. Nina wasn't like the other mothers in Merseyside. She had it together. Nina owned a flower shop in North Jersey and was active in her son's treatment and recovery.

Billy was a junkie, doing anything from PCP to shooting dope, he loved drugs. I never thought what a child's actions could have on their parents' psyche until I met Nina, and saw how much she loved her son, even though he was a constant disappointment. She held out hope for sunnier days, but it just kept raining angst, sorrow, and anxiety. The constant barrage of frenzy was leading her to die a little more inside every time Billy would pull his shit and fuck up.

Nina and my mom's relationship only grew from that point on, attending Merseysides weekly support groups together. Their relationship evolved to chatting on email and the phone. They used each other as crutches of strength in difficult times.

While taking on Billy as my understudy provided me with a window into this kids mind and method of operation. I could never understand Billy and his reason for self-destruction when things seemed to just be turning the corner for him.

Yet just when you'd want to throw in the towel, giving up hope for the kid, he does something that makes you stop and scratch your head in amazement, staying one step ahead of me, always finding ways to trigger me into staying invested in him.

Billy has swings like the stock market, some weeks he's up, other he's down in terms of performance. He was getting "shot down" every week for about two months, getting in trouble for petty infractions. He loved to steal bread and cheese from the kitchen to grill on the burning hot radiators in our rooms. *Ghetto as fuck, I know.*

Brian on the other hand, portrayed this squeaky clean image but had an affinity for smashing fat chicks in Merseyside and swigging hand sanitizer mixed with juice as a way to get drunk. He was so sly and sneaky, he never drew attention to himself. In Merseyside terms,

"His Belly (conscious) is Filthy. He has MAD guilt."

Unlike Brian, Billy did things to get attention. Always craving it, and when he wouldn't get it, he would rev up the stakes to make sure he got everybody's attention. Billy had finally gotten approved for a request, a nine hour home visit with a buddy, which would have been me, but Billy didn't want to go that week, so to get his request pulled, he marched into the dining room at breakfast time while everyone was eating. Prettifying everybody only his boxers, Billy points to the writing printed on the front of his shorts with an arrow pointing down.

"Don't be shy, step right up, take a peek at my Lock Ness Monster."

Needless to say, Billy didn't go home that week.

Brian and Billy really made stay there tolerable. They both made me laugh and felt like real friends. I held them both to the same regard. Although I trusted Billy slightly more than Brian, I was becoming closer to Billy, but kept Brian just as close. He lived near me on the outside and figured we could have a legitimate friendship.

Normally I wouldn't think twice to want to meet any of these people on the outside. I sincerely wanted to become something more, and not stew in my own shit any longer, so I didn't want my new life to intersect with my old one. But Brian and I had a common bond that neither of us knew until Pastor Dan came to visit me again. Pastor Dan is from Brian's' town, and knows him very well.

When Pastor Dan would spend time with me, he'd also see Brian, and talk to us both. Recognizing that we have each other to lean on would lead to a deeper bond and better chance at success. This also took my relationship with Brian to a new level, a spiritual understanding of one another. This allowed me to trust Brian, and love him like a brother.

It was now mid-November and Billy was finally going on his first request. Brian had gone on two already and was advancing nicely in the program. I had my eye on the prize and knew I only had a little while longer. Collette promised me as long as Billy's request went smoothly, when I came back she would sit down with me and talk about completion and pick a date for me to finally go home.

Her statement was littered with irony, she was pinning my hope of freedom on a successful request with Billy, ultimately putting my future in the hands of Porky the Pig. That meant no cigarettes, coffee, sex, drugs, illegal friend contact, deviation from written and approved itinerary and following any of the other plethora of rules Merseyside had.

The night before my trip with Billy, I laid out the ground rules on what I would and wouldn't play ball on. I didn't care about friends and cigarettes, as I routinely smoked massive amounts of cigarettes when I was home, usually driving around in my car drinking coffee while downing cancer sticks at world record pace.

I just wouldn't tolerate any drug use, besides the obvious reasons of not getting high, Merseyside drug tests everybody and a positive drug test for either Billy or I meant the chair, and more importantly to me, the delay of my completion.

I thought I was in the clear and could enjoy the night and the day tomorrow of having Billy's mom cook us a mouthwatering Italian dinner, washing it down with some Coca-Cola, watching TV and taking in the sights and sounds of reality. Until Billy tells me, in a very nonchalant, oh by the way type of attitude,

"Yeah Lucas, I have about **ten bags of dope under my bed**, along with two syringes and a spoon."

I retreated back to my room with my heart in my stomach, knowing that resisting heroin for smack addicts is like trying to deny a pit bull a porterhouse steak, almost impossible and can get vicious. I turned out the lights on the day that night obsessing over the fact that if I take my eyes off of Billy for thirty seconds, he'll probably get high. Billy getting high means my completion date will get delayed. I didn't have much confidence in

Billy's self-control, but was determined not to let Porky oink this up for me.

CHAPTER 16

Heroin Sheik

Think about it, would you put faith in a heroin addict? So needless to say I had very little faith Billy would actually not try and look for his stash.

Like I said though he had a likeable quality about him that was hard to ignore, after all, I felt it was my mission to help this kid, it kind of was but I saw my mom's pain magnified one hundred times in Billy's mom's eyes. Nina and my ma were very similar. As time went on, I realized how similar Billy and I were.

Yeah, I thought he was slow, or had some kind of mental problem, but our actions were strikingly similar. We both enjoyed totally blowing the fuck up. The hardest part for people like us was building a foundation and nurturing it until it was complete. We made the same mistakes, but on a different scale. It's a sobering reality. Recognizing you are the person who's sitting in the front seat, just a little bit luckier.

My deep thinking brain trance had made me totally forgot about the ten bags of heroin in Billy's room.

My concentration was finally broken when Billy unleashed his inner Ricky Ricardo and belted,

"Oh, Lucy, I'm HOME."

His mother and grandmother owned a flower shop downstairs, and they resided upstairs. The outside greeted you with lattices dressed up with ivy, two big windows stuffed filled with tulips, Roses and beautifully colored and crafted bouquets. A big cut-out red rose was the store's signage with the name *"A PERCULIAR FLOWER"* sitting below it. We all walked into the front of the shop to surprise his "Nanna."

She thought the world of Billy and wasn't at the point with him that Nina was. Just entering you're blasted with the scent of fresh cut flowers and the feeling of mist.

Billy snuck up on Nanna trying to give her the "ultimate" surprise as he called it. And in the process almost gave the poor lady a heart attack, I guess her being eighty seven didn't register with Porky.

I was more focused on the marinara sauce she had going on the stove, and the macaroni ready to be thrown into the boiling pot of water. The smell of fresh bread replaced the scent of flowers, my stomach was now dictating to my brain. It was saying, FEED ME!

Good food was hard to come by now a days, let alone food that rivaled my mom's home cooking. Nina was also quite the chef, and I had been hearing about this epic feast for a week now. I was salivating staring at what was about to fill my stomach. I never set the table, but I did this time in hopes we would eat sooner. Before we sat down to dig in, Billy's mom said grace, and not one of hymns and vague meanings, she was direct.

" *Lord, please bring me more of these meals with my family, help my son, let him do good, please, please Lord I beg you let this be the last time, I miss and need my son, and don't know how much more I can take, I love you and thank you for these opportunities you present us with. Amen.*"

Dinner was served.

After eating three thousand calories, most of them carbs, I found myself in a heavy food coma on the couch in the living room. Nina and Nanna weren't around, Billy was trolling around in his room getting changed.

You know that inner voice inside your head? Not the, I'm a schizophrenic voice, but the HEY BUDDY, SOMETHING'S NOT RIGHT voice. Well I listened to it and got my fat ass off the couch and opened the door to Billy's room.

He was sitting on his bed. Ten bags of dope beside him and a syringe with a spoon in his lap. I uttered something stupid, probably along the lines of *bro what the fuck are you doing.*

He shrugged it off though. He was looking past me, and past the walls, into no man's lands. It was silent for about a minute, we were both quiet.

"You know Lucas, everyone thinks I'm going to fuck up again because I want too, but I don't. I was like you, just deep enough to where I could pull myself out. But if you keep on digging that hole, eventually it just makes more sense to keep going until you reach the other side. It's closer than turning around and starting over. "

I felt the ghosts that were swept under the rug while he was gone. The same flower shop he called home was the same place that would be providing his floral arraigments for his funeral. Billy knew he was on the fast track to die, and no matter how much he loved his mom, or his life and the possibility of a happy ending, he was in so deep he knew it could never be the same again. He gave up trying.

"But Lucas, I won't start digging on your watch."

He grabbed his syringe and spoon, and ordered me to take the dope and follow him to the bathroom. It was all of ten steps to the toilet, but felt like three miles. Before I could even start to freak out, Billy snapped the syringe and knocked the dope out of my hand and into the toilet and flushed it. It was over.

Billy was biting his lip so hard he made himself bleed. I told him I loved him. That was probably one of the balls-ist things I've ever seen someone do.

Billy started to cry, reaching for me to hug him. He told me.

"Lucas, I don't want to die."

I wish there was more to tell about that day. Besides smoking a few cigarettes and meeting Billy's dad, I left knowing my friend would never be ok.

CHAPTER 17

Tight House.

My intuition was dead on. After the results came back from mine and Billy's drug tests negative. I was promoted to re-entry, the last phase of Merseyside.

Re-entry is Merseyside's way of dangling the carrot of going home even closer to your face. They give you more freedom and less structure. They are basically trying to trap you into fucking up so you can stay in the system longer. Still though, it was a much better deal than what the rest of the house got.

When I mentioned earlier some kids had been in Merseyside for years? Well this is where they reside. I had to be careful to not become one of those ghosts. I saw firsthand how an eight month stay could turn into two years and that wasn't going to be me pal.

I knew that the only other thing that could fuck me was a tight house.

Tight house is another Merseyside term. It means that nobody has any privileges. They make you clean the house morning to night and don't let anyone talk or make a sound for days. The residents are forced to drop guilt and fess up to their rule breaking. Confess a cardinal sin, chances are they leave you on the chair for days. In tight houses, Merseyside will send kids back to prison if they have really filthy guilt. This is how Merseyside regains and keeps control.

The part that does me in though is the little caveat that states **NOBODY GOES HOME.**

No requests, special permissions, or completions . . . yes, completions. Fuck.

For now though, I was enjoying re-entry waiting for the holidays to pass while keeping a low profile earned me the **target completion date of January 7ᵗʰ.**

As happy as I was, I knew it was a set up. It's hard to fool ninety drug addicts in a small house. Word had gotten out about the infamous tight house. Focus had shifted to when and not if.

Christmas came and went. And spending New Year's Eve in a sober living facility is very awkward. What was worse than watching starving inmates salivating over Chinese food they haven't eaten in about a year was the fact when we woke up tomorrow were all fucked. **January 1ˢᵗ. Ion was coming.**

Whose Ion you ask? Ion is the big swinging dick that runs all the Merseysides on the east coast. I found out who Ion was at 6 AM on January 1ˢᵗ when we were all woken up by the staff banging pots and pans, ordering us to go downstairs into the gym.

We were all greeted by a gum chewing napoleon complex that was British and rude as fuck.

"My name is Ion, I'm here to tell you people. You're all in a fucking *TIGHT HOUSE*."

Just like that he said it. You could hear everyone's assholes pucker around the room. We were all handed a cheap yellow pad and pen. The guilt dropping started immediately. People were scared and dropping like flies. A lot of snitching went on that morning.

My only concern was whether I was still going home or not.

I barely had any guilt with the other cellies. Besides a few cigarettes smoked and unsanctioned girlfriend visits, I was clean. Honestly, during the last part of re-entry, I started getting wasted on request with my old high school friends. But I wasn't stupid enough to tell anybody that.

I knew I wasn't going to know about January 7th until the day of or night before. Only because Collette and Merseyside wanted to read all the guilt first to make sure I wasn't indicated in any of it. Also since the place was on lock down, I wasn't going to be able to get alone time with Collette or even have contact with my family.

Let me explain, in detail what exactly a tight house is and what they do to you in it.

First off, every morning you wake up at 4 am to the staff banging pots and pans, screaming at you. You must remain silent from the moment you wake up to the instant you fall asleep.

After eating breakfast in the dark, with only the sound of people chewing cereal you start the day. It's fucking hell.

I mentioned the hours of cleaning earlier. But you are literally on your hands and knees scrubbing for dear life while the slave masters, I mean counselors, prowl above you hurling antagonistic remarks with the sole intention to break you.

At Merseyside, they want to crush you. *It's the only way you can get better. Don't you know that?*

After hours of cleaning, we were ordered back into seats where we would then drop more guilt until dinner time. Merseyside doesn't expect drug addicts to come clean on their own. So they would round up the most innocent. Usually I was a part of this group, and force us to interrogate one of our peers. This is called a **HAIRCUT.**

A Haircut consists of three to four Merseysiders and a counselor grilling the shit out of a flunky. The one being put on blast sits on a metal chair while the four of us circle him/her. Our only job was to get them to confess and render a verdict. It was pretty vicious sometimes. I was a total sell out too. I did whatever it took to get me the fuck out of there.

The cleaning. The yelling. The silence. All of it was a ground hogs day event. 4am to 10pm. Every single fucking minute of the day.

The thing about a tight house is, you never know how long they can last for. They don't have set end dates. Merseyside has been known to keep the house tight for weeks, even months. It was going on day five and I was already over it.

My completion date was two

days away. I still hadn't talked to Collette or my parents. I was freaking out. I felt like I was about to be stopped on the 1 yard line with the game clock expiring.

That night, I caught a huge fucking break. I caught one of the other re-Entry kids with a cell phone. No way was I ratting on him.

Instead I used it to call my parents. As childish as it sounds, Mommy and Daddy saved me.

I told them how shit had hit the fan and how we were on lockdown. Now I had to be Joe Cool with this because Merseyside couldn't find out I spoke with my parents, especially on a smuggled cell phone. I told them to play dumb and call in the morning to confirm my departure. Any push back on the date, say I'm already enrolled in school and expected to start that Monday.

I hung up the phone knowing I unleashed a little bit of my inner Lex Luther but I had to get the fuck out of this place. **I knew all along I had no plans to change.**

I might have thought I did, but really I saw this whole experience juvie and Merseyside as one big obstacle in my way to ultimately doing what I want. I got smarter along the way and matured in the process.

If the ends justify the means, then all I really wanted was to get on with my life. Fuck the self-help bullshit. I wasn't even a drug addict. I was just a clumsy sociopath.

CHAPTER 18

Exit Stage Left

Completion Day is a sacred thing around Merseyside.

The house gathers in the auditorium and your family and friends are there to watch you walk in to a room full of cheers and hear members of the staff and fellow residents say nice things about you. It's actually very touching and I always wanted my own.

I hated sitting through everyone else's. Watching other people complete sucked. I would sit there knowing the person I was watching talk was probably going to relapse within a week. I didn't wish that on them, but the odds are really stacked against you with certain drugs. That didn't bother me though. What pissed me off the most was when the ceremony ended

Seeing that person happy drove me nuts. They were on the other side of the wall. They were free and I was not. I wanted what they had.

So when I would walk by them, I would say. **Congratulations**, but inside I was saying **Fuck you**. You lucky bastard.

As sacred as completion day was and no matter how much I wanted my own ceremony. I was willing to settle for nothing just get out of there on January 7th.

I wish I could remember how I felt the day before. It was all a blur until Collette called me into her office around 6 pm while the residents were downstairs eating. I was either about to roll 7's or snake eyes.

Collette's cold bitch face stared me down before telling me.

As much as I think you need more treatment and think you need this more than you think. You are going home tomorrow.

Jack fucking pot.

She went on to say.

You are by no means to share this information with anyone. You are not extended a completion ceremony at this time due to tight house conditions. Your scheduled release is for 9 am tomorrow morning. Have your bag packed and keep your goodbyes limited and discreet. Again, this is a tight house. This doesn't happen.

I win was the first thought I had. Followed by *Fuck you Merseyside*.

The hardest part now was trying not to look so happy while everyone else looked so miserable.

I didn't even sleep that night. I packed my bag and waited patiently for the morning. There was a general shadiness about me completing but I mean that's Merseyside. They are the sneakiest mother fuckers around. I learned a lot from them in that regard.

Around 8 am the following morning word had gotten out that I was going home. I was met with more *fuck you's* and *you're a lucky bastard* comments than *congratulations* and *good luck's*. Trust me I get it.

I only said goodbye to three people; Lauren, Brian, and Billy. It wasn't because I didn't like anyone else there. I just knew those three would be the only people I might see beyond these walls. Everyone else was just a rehab friend.

I walked out the front door of Merseyside Village at 9:01 am. January 7th.

Just like that. It was over. I thought there would be more of a buildup or exhilaration inside of me. Instead it was very anti climatic. Freedom didn't hit me like I thought it would. I just drifted away.

CHAPTER 19

Full Circle

Sometimes life doesn't give us the happy endings we were expecting. To tell you I became an all-Star member of society would be a great lie. As much as I lie, this isn't.

I was released by Merseyside at 9am January 7th. I got stoned and almost arrested less than twelve hours later. I was going to take an L cruise around the old neighborhood to celebrate my release. Before I could even spark the blunt, I was pulled over and searched. The officer didn't find the pot, but he did say,

Welcome back Mancini.

That night, I got so high, I threw up all over my mom's living room and passed out half naked on the couch. The next day, I missed my first day of school. It was happening all over again.

What made it worse was I was still on probation until that May. So I had Merseyside Out Patient, Probation, my parents, and my high school all drug testing me up my ass.

I didn't care. I was going to do my thing. I hate authority. Not like fuck the police necessarily. But my rational can be a dangerous place and I hate being told what to do. Whatever the case, I was fucking myself again.

When I did finally get my ass to school for my first day back they told me I was being held back. I was still a junior. Fuck me man. The stigma of that burned. My pride made me feel like a retard. That embarrassment enraged me.

All my old friends who despised me before I left welcomed me back. Although they were afraid my experience had permanently fucked me up, I presume they only admitted that to me after the fact they saw I was still "on their level."

Their friendship didn't last long though. About a week later, a party of theirs got raided and they thought I ratted them out to the cops. Seriously. Imagine reading the headline.

Cops bust Abercrombie & Fitch wearing teens drinking in their parent's basement, an eight month investigation concludes.

Gimme a fuckin' break. A week after that, I got jumped by two separate people I had robbed the year prior. Revenge is a mother fucker.

In the three weeks I had been home, I got into two fights, skipped a week of school and failed two consecutive drug tests. I was about to go away again.

As for my other friends, Stan, Danny, and Pita? They were junkies at this point. Pita, who was the smartest of all of them, was also selling heroin. While their lives were a continuing train wreck, mine was heading back onto the collision course.

I was home for thirty days before I violated probation and was officially kicked out of school, again.

I thought my life was over at this point. Until Pastor Dan saved me.

It's true. He talked to the judge at my probation violation hearing. Instead of jail for my eighteenth birthday, I was accepted into the Recovery Institute of South Florida, a halfway house for adults. That was all because of Pastor Dan. My future had been pardoned. I was given one last chance to make this right.

And I did.

I left Florida off probation and arrived home to a clean slate. My past was gone. My old friends graduated high school and went off to college. The others were either dead from drugs or in jail because of them.

I was a chubby 18 year old who got another chance to make a better life for myself. My juvenile record was sealed. I got my G.E.D and enrolled in community college. I even went and got a real job, at an old women's shoe store.

Life is what we make of it. I was a total scumbag for what I did to other people and what I did to myself. I had to make a choice. *Is this how I wanted to live?*

I attended quite a few funerals for people I knew in Merseyside. They were right about one thing, Merseyside. Most of us did end up dead or in jail. Billy is in prison. Brian committed suicide and I don't know what happened to Lauren.

I called Pastor Dan after work one day to thank him for everything. His wife picked up and told me the news. He was dead.

Pastor Dan died a few months after I got home from Florida. He had a late stage aggressive cancer. He was dead two months after they found it. I never got to say goodbye to the man that saved my life.

In the end. My father might have been onto something that night when he called me a lucky bastard many moons ago while playing Monopoly in the kitchen. Ever since the first time. People have used many variations telling me the exact same thing.

It strokes and insults your ego all at the same time. I feel like it's a dirty way of saying *Good Job*.

To me, in all phases of luck. There is nothing luckier than being able to have another chance. It's the offer of redemption. So the next time somebody calls you lucky, appreciate it. No matter what form it comes in.

LUCKY B*STARD

29375570R00150

Made in the USA
Middletown, DE
17 February 2016